PRAISE FOR WILLIAM GAY'S WORK

Little Sister Death

"Chilling, beautiful, quietly shocking ... a study of the writer: his temperament, his torment, and his devil's pact for the price of a good story."
—*The Independent*

"*Little Sister Death* is not a glib meat-commentary on horror ... but a personal glimpse at Gay's own life, at the way a dedicated artist does not exorcise his demons—but seeks them out, and invites them in."
—*Electric Lit*

"Gay's signature muscular prose, authentic dialogue, and vivid setting combine to make this posthumous novel a worthwhile read."
—*Publishers Weekly*

"Cannily crafted, exceptional in its storytelling and doubly seductive in its sultry Southern setting ... *Little Sister Death* is literary horror of the highest order."
—*Tor.com*

"Gay takes the familiar trope of the haunted house and imbues it with a slow-burning melancholy and a sense of the inescapability of fate."
—*Big Issue*

"If you mix Stephen King with William Faulkner, the result would be the posthumous novel *Little Sister Death* by William Gay ... a great read for a quiet night at home, in an empty house, with the lights off except for a lone reading lamp."
—*The Knoxville News Sentinel*

The Long Home

"Gay has created a novel of great emotional power."
—*Denver Post*

"It'll leave you breathless ..."
—*Rocky Mountain News*

Provinces of Night

"Earthily idiosyncratic, spookily gothic ... an author with a powerful vision."
—*The New York Times*

"An extremely seductive read."
—*Washington Post Book World*

"Southern writing at its very finest, soaked through with the words and images of rural Tennessee, packed full of that which really matters, the problems of the human heart."
—*Booklist*

"A writer of striking talent."
—*Chicago Tribune*

"Almost a personal revival of handwork in fiction — superb—must be listened to and felt."
—*Barry Hannah, Geronimo Rex* and *Airships*

"This is a novel from the old school. The characters are truly characters. The prose is gothic. And the charm is big."
—*The San Diego Union-Tribune*

"Writers like Flannery O'Connor or William Faulkner would welcome Gay as their peer for getting characters so entangled in the roots of a family tree."
—*Star Tribune (Minneapolis)*

". . . the preciousness of hope, the fragility of dreams, interwoven with a good-size dollop of Biblical justice and the belief that a Southern family can be cursed."
—*The Miami Herald*

"Plumbs the larger things in life … The epic and the personal unite seamlessly."
—*Milwaukee Journal Sentinel*

"An old-fashioned barrel-aged shot of Tennessee story-telling. Gay's tale of ancient wrongs and men with guns is high-proof stuff."
—Elwood Reid, *Midnight Sun* and *What Salmon Know*

"A finely wrought, moving story with a plot as old as Homer. Sometimes the old ones are the best ones."
—*The Atlanta Journal Constitution*

"William Gay is the big new name to include in the storied annals of Southern lit."
—*Esquire*

"A plot so gripping that the reader wants to fly through the pages to reach the conclusion … but the beauty and richness of Gay's language exerts a contrary pull, making the reader want to linger over every word."
—*Rocky Mountain News*

"Gay is a terrific writer."
—*The Plain Dealer*

Twilight

"Think *No Country for Old Men* by Cormac McCarthy and *Deliverance* by James Dickey ... then double the impact."
—*Stephen King*

"There is much to admire here: breathtaking, evocative writing and a dark, sardonic humor."
—*USA Today*

"William Gay brings the daring of Flannery O'Connor and William Gaddis to his lush and violent surrealist yarns."
—*The Irish Times*

"This is Southern Gothic of the very darkest hue, dripping with atmosphere, sparkling with loquacity, and with occasional gleams of horrible humor. To be read in the broadest daylight."
—*The Times*

I Hate to See that Evening Sun Go Down

"William Gay is richly gifted: a seemingly effortless storyteller ... a writer of prose that's fiercely wrought, pungent in detail yet poetic in the most welcome sense."
—*The New York Times Book Review*

'One perfect tale follows another, leaving you in little doubt that Gay is a genuine poet of the ornery, the estranged, the disenfranchised, crafting stories meant to last."
—*Seattle Times*

FUGITIVES

OF THE

HEART

WILLIAM GAY

Livingston Press
The University of West Alabama

ISBN 978-1-60489-273-4, hardcover

Library of Congress Control Number: 2021930553
Gay, William Ebert, 1939 - 2012

Compiled and edited by J. M. White
With editorial assistance from: Shelia Kennedy, Susan McDonald, Lamont Ingalls, Paul Nitsche, Matt Snope, Coree Entwistle, Dawn Major and George Dilworth.

Typesetting and page layout: Joe Taylor
Proofreading: Joe Taylor, Mason Pendergrass, Nic Nolin, Evan Jones
Cover Design: Joe Taylor
Front Cover Photo: J. M. White
Cover Painting: William Gay
Author Photo: J. M. White

TABLE OF CONTENTS

There is nothing that is a thing to itself, Crowe told him. No event stands alone, separate from all other events. Everything that happens is influenced by what came before and it in its turn influences what comes after.

There's a difference between being tough and just not giving a shit.

Not Enough Knuckles

Sonny Brewer

I was there when William Gay discovered somebody
had broken into his trailer and vandalized the place. He
walked in to find a wreck and the back door still ajar.
His trailer sat on a pretty little rise on Grinder's Creek Road
outside of Hohenwald, Tennessee, where William lived
with his Pitbull, Knuckles. But Knuckles was missing in
action the day the thief hit and I didn't think to ask William about his good dog until days later back home in
Fairhope, Alabama.

Best I can remember — Lord, how the years pile up
behind me — it was in 2001 when the break-in happened.
I had left Fairhope driving the company vehicle for my
Over the Transom Bookstore, a maroon Chevy Astro
van, for a little trip with William to a book conference.
The ride was not nearly as cushy as the Mercury Marquis
Brougham — a first cousin to a Lincoln Town Car — that
I would rent nine years later to make a 2700-mile round
trip from Hohenwald to Waterville, Maine, with William
for his reading and talk at Colby College. Me and William, we made lots of roadtrips.

William was sitting on his porch ready when I drove
up. He loaded his bag and we pulled out of his drive on
a rainy October weekend heading for Memphis and the
Southern Independent Booksellers' Association weekend,
a trade show that we rarely missed.

After we checked in to the hotel, we wandered outside and walked to Beale Street.

The rain had stopped and it was crazy crowded on
Beale. We dodged people on the sidewalk and in the street

looking for a place to grab a beer. Every bar was packed. We kept walking, watching the show. A pale goth chick all in black, with long straight black hair and multiple piercings, broke her stride to launch into a series of somersaults down the middle of the street. No one seemed to notice, but it was enough for William: "You ready to head back to the hotel? This looks like a dress rehearsal for hell." We turned and retraced our steps out of there.

The readings and panels were good, but a funk hung over the weekend. The mood was a mix of numb and edgy from the terrorist attacks on September 11th a little over three weeks earlier. By Sunday, we were both ready to get home. We had some coffee and Bloody Marys at the hotel and gathered up our strength and made the haul back down to Grinder's Creek — we were both like little wrinkled party balloons (thanks for the image Paul Simon). So when we rolled up to the trailer, I'd already told William I was not going to hang out. I meant to just keep the van in gear in his driveway, foot on the brake, idling, and soon as he and his bag were clear, find the gas pedal, man-up and get on back down the highway.

Last time William and I wrapped up a road trip, winding up back at his place on a Sunday afternoon, we had sat on the side porch and listened to some music and talked. William's son Chris was there and played his guitar and sang some original songs. Whiskey was passed around. I'd rolled out in time to make the seven-hour ride to Fairhope before midnight. But not this time.

Anyway, in a month I'd be hosting Southern Writers Reading in Fairhope and William would come down for that. The energy would be much better.

I dropped off William, and pulled away. I was down the driveway not yet clear of the loose gravel, hadn't made it to the blacktop highway out front, when I looked in the rearview mirror and saw him step out and raise his arm. If I'd come home to what he'd just seen, I'd be flapping both arms like a drunken sailor. William was not like that, not given to histrionics.

I wondered, what the hell? I slowly backed up. I stopped and let down the window on the passenger side.

Somebody broke in, he said.

I forgot I was gutshot tired and jumped out of the van, following him inside. William led me through the mess to the back door that was swung back, standing wide open. He stepped aside so I could see hundreds of music CDs and movie DVDs slung down that fair and wooded hillside leading away from the trailer.

Damn, man. Who'd do this? I asked.

I got my ideas, he said.

You mean somebody you know? He nodded. They take anything?

Yeah. A box of writing. That at least. I don't yet know what else.

What the hell? Stories?

Stories and a book about the bloody days on the Natchez Trace.

You mean a complete novel?

Yeah.

I sat down on the couch. William was struck quiet. He lit a cigarette. So, when you're dead and gone, we'll see a William Gay novel that was mysteriously found?

I don't much think so. It was longhand in notebooks. Maybe broken up by other stories. Maybe some scene meant for something else. I don't think anybody but me could piece it all together right.

Okay, that's been proven wrong.

Michael White and his team spent many painstaking hours over months "piecing together" one at a time the four novels that came to light after William's death: *The Lost Country, Little Sister Death, Stoneburner* and now this one, *Fugitives of the Heart.*

I asked Michael, of course, if among the tubs of holographic manuscript pages they worked on did he come up with anything on the Natchez Trace. "Yes," he said, "but it's only a fragment. Not an entire novel, by any means. Not even close." And it was then that I told him of the day of the break-in at the trailer. He said he knew about that. I told him what William said to me, that he'd finished the novel on the Natchez Trace, that we'd even talked about its unlikely posthumous publication. Michael said that he wasn't so sure William actually completed the manuscript. I believe otherwise.

I left William that day, concerned about what might come of the bad scene he'd come home to. When I called to check on him later in the week, I brought up Knuckles.

That bad dog you've got, where was he when somebody came in your place?

Knuckles is not a fighter, I reckon. I expect he was off rambling around someplace looking for love.

Where's a good bad dog when you need him, I asked, and told William I'd better get back to work. I was behind the counter in my bookstore, greeting customers and working on plans for the third annual Southern Writers Reading. A literary slugfest, as Jim Gilbert called it, though no fists would be thrown in the company of such a cultured crowd in attendance. Just a big party and celebration of the best of Southern authors that would run for a dozen years and became a huge event, drawing writers from all over the country, mostly expat Southerners.

A little over a month later, in November the weekend before Thanksgiving, same time every year in all of its years, the show was set to crank up on a Thursday night.

I borrowed the Theatre 98 playhouse as our venue for the author readings and onstage interviews. William had helped me initiate the series in 1999, appearing with writers Frank Turner Hollon and Tom Franklin. By this the third season, William's first novel had come out and he was the Bob Dylan-looking rock star in the ghosted halls of Southern lit. This year William would be our headliner, opening the weekend with a Thursday night reading, then doing another on Saturday night

When it was getting close to show time, it turned out I was too busy with last minute details to go up to Grinder's Creek and fetch this genius who did not like to merge or drive over bridges and so just quit the driving business altogether—hence all our roadtrips. Mind you, I dearly loved to be behind the wheel, but I had to send somebody after William. Drive up, get him, and bring him to Fairhope, then I'd take him home.

And when I sat down to write this, I damn well could not remember who went to get William for me. But, whoever stepped up, I want to believe having William Gay ride shotgun was worth all the trouble. You can't spend seven hours in a car with William and not come out ahead on the transaction.

Problem was, the program had to kick off without William because they were running late. I took the microphone a couple of times as the authors finished their readings to say William would surely show up soon.

And when they finally arrived, the driver and William, the door at the back of the theater busted open and it was like one of those backlit silhouette moments in the movies, rousing applause as he slow-walked down the aisle between the jam-packed seats, this Tennessee writer that Stephen King called an American treasure laboring at his art in obscurity in the hills of East Tennessee. This night, he was anything but obscure. I don't remember who was in the middle of their reading when William arrived, but they knew they'd been tagged and stepped away from the mic for Mr. Gay to take over the evening. He needed no introduction.

When William Gay died in 2012, Jim Gilbert my former bookstore manager wrote the obituary for *The Mobile Press Register* newspaper:

"While his themes are not exactly the stuff of musical comedies, his prose is not without levity, often downright hilarity. At the 2001 session of Fairhope's literary Southern Writers Reading series, Gay brought down the house reading a scene from *Provinces of Night* about two men using bricks to secure a blow-up doll beside a rural mailbox. (And for those fortunate enough to have heard Gay read his work aloud, it is impossible to view his words upon a page — whether crafted prose or an off-the-cuff answer to an interview question — without hearing his distinctive Tennessee drawl, more personal than merely Southern, so rich as to have often seemed like a language unto itself.) He was a master at what Bram Stoker referred to in *Dracula* as the King Laugh — 'things are never so terrible that human beings will cease to find humor. Not, at least, without ceasing to be human.'"

So William owned the room that night. Brought the house down, as Jim said. But he could do that without effort—no swagger, no phony ego strutting. Let me, in fact, recall here how Professor Cedric Bryant introduced William Gay to the audience that we drove to Maine to find there at Colby College: "This evening was originally planned for last spring when William Gay, who neither drives nor flies much, informed us that a friend might drive him to Maine...As time passed, the great possibility of getting William Gay to Colby began to seem to me like, well, a Samuel Beckett play, in which all of us were perfectly willing captives just waiting…! And now that everybody is here this evening in our very special Robinson Room, it seems perfectly clear that Miguel Cervantes was wrong: when one is waiting for William Gay, at least, it is certainly not 'better to travel than to have arrived.'

Dr. Bryant continued, "William Gay writes about the possibility of redemption and the shattering realization of its limitations. The real, hard scrabble life in Gay's novels and stories often begins at the borderlands of old age and haunted memory, where all questions about living and dying have been exhausted, save one: whether to go on or not? There is a ruthless realism—call it the Southern Gothic, if you like—where the absurdly comic world of busted crimpers and reports of a man kidnapped off a Greyhound bus by four girls from a Baptist youth camp—who 'have their way with him'—collides with the grotesque gift of a frozen baby and reveals to its grieving mother, the paradoxical nature of crime, miracles, and punishment."

And it was this man's work that had been stolen that weekend twenty years back—the crime of depriving us of a William Gay novel, that lacks so far a miracle of discovery, or punishment that we know of, though there exists the possibility of a haunted mind for the thief. Or that Knuckles went rambling and settled a score.

Jim Dees in Oxford, Mississippi, host of *Thacker Mountain Radio*, edited a collection that he called *They Write Among Us*, and, William was included among those Oxford writers, even though William did not live in Oxford. But he loved the town and its heritage as a "hotbed of literary talent" and the town loved him back. William was included because he more than held his own in that good company of fine writers.

William wrote a piece that I published in the anthology *Don't Quit Your Day Job* about the soul-marked turn he made to become a writer: "I had no words for the way the snow looked drifting down in the streetlights and I wanted those words. If they were anywhere I would find them." We who read William Gay know he found the words, and that he could use them on white drifting snow or red bloodletting in the Harrikin, and use the words better than anybody.

It's a damn shame that William Gay no longer writes among us.

And it's a thing with feathers in our hearts that maybe, one more time, after this book you have in your hands, the Natchez Trace novel from William will be found and published. And I will not say to Michael White, I told you so.

BOOK ONE

ALLEN'S CREEK

Yates's father's sole claim to immortality was that he used to cause good car wrecks. On Allen's Creek, there's a steep curve overlooked by a red clay bank and on the other side a precipitous cliff attended by an illusory border of delicate alders. If you don't negotiate the curve you go down through the alders to the tables of limestone, who knows how far, farther than you'd want to go. Yates's father had a long blonde frightwig he'd come by somewhere and a short red dress and he used to paint his mouth gaudily with fire red lipstick, mascara his eyes and whiten his cheeks with rice powder and go sit atop the clay bank overlooking the road. Skirt hiked and awaiting the unwary, shaven legs spread lasciviously. An ungodly sight, nightmarish, perhaps from hell, some displaced flapper from another time, another place. It is told by some old-timers that he wore women's underwear when he did this, black some say, or red. Others debate it, fact as well as color. A sense of humor is a sense of humor, but pulling on a pair of women's drawers is another thing altogether. His best day was early in the summer of 1941 when he sent a rattletrap Plymouth loaded with drunks end over end to their doom. Three were killed outright and two more died in the hospital. Afterwards a survivor said, That was either a man wearing a dress or the ugliest white woman I have ever seen.

Other than his sense of humor he had no saving graces, he was a drunk and he was lazy. He was a drunk only when he could get whiskey but he was lazy all the time. He had a job breaking ore in the mine, but a fifty-pound sledgehammer grows ever heavier when the morrow is as bleak as today, and ultimately he turned to stealing and that was his undoing.

The boy was awakened in the winter's night by the creak of a wagon, the rattling of traces, iron wheels turning in frozen snow, the wind at the eaves tinkling the loose windowpanes in their sashes like chimes. He was instantly awake. Sany Claus?, he thought. He was up, bare feet on the cold floor. He crossed silent to the nearest window. There was a wagon and a team of mules, their steaming breath pluming palely. There were voices. He went out.

There was moonlight, a few ragged skiffs of snow, white against the black of the frozen night. It was very cold.

What is it? his mother asked. There was an undercurrent of terror in her voice. She had an old overcoat clutched about her.

Fresh meat, by God, the man in the wagon said. His voice was muffled by effort. He leant and straightened and rolled over the sideboards a man's body that fell slackly and moved once when it struck the frozen earth then no more.

The woman knelt over it there on the frozen snow. Her breath made a kind of keening whistling sound. The woman straightened and turned. Her face was ravaged and broken. The blood covering her hands and face looked black in the moonlight. She turned toward the boy but she didn't seem to see him. She approached the wagon.

I told him three times is just two too many, the man said. I aimed to fire over his head but he's a purty tall feller and a little taller than I took him to be.

From the high wagonseat he looked as big as God. I told it around, whoever's been hittin my smokehouse would be toted off when I caught em. Well here he is. I caught him.

You son of a bitch, the woman said. You lowlife son of a bitch.

It's hard times, the man said, just stating a fact, and it takes hard people to get through em. I got mouths of my own to feed. You don't have to go to no law. I'm goin to the high sheriff myself and tell him what I done. But I wouldn't expect much if I were you. Thieves was never thought much of in this part of the county.

The boy felt this was not to be borne. It ain't real, he thought, none of it. I'm dreamin it. It ain't real because nobody could stand this. If it was real I'd die in a heartbeat till I was deader than him, I'd disappear like smoke and be just as gone. I can't stand this.

The man snapped the lines and the wagon wheeled about in the dirty snow then he abruptly halted the mules. He picked up something else and rolled it over the sideboards. It looked like a side of meat. I'm a fair man, the man said. His face was grizzled with thin gray whiskers, he turned his head to spit amber onto the yard. If he wanted it bad enough to trade his life for it then it's hisn. I am fair and you welcome to it. I figure it's paid for. He turned to acknowledge the boy. Beneath the moonlit shadow of the slouch hat his face appeared masked. A likely boy should learn somethin from this, he said.

She swore they'd not touch a bite of the meat but like he said times was hard and in the end they did. A secret fear nagged at him. He wondered had there been blood on the meat but he didn't dare ask. He wondered if there was had she cut it off, but he didn't ask that either.

Winter that year was short and mild. Then a false spring came in late February and overnight the world softly altered. First the softwoods then the oak and hickory budded and sprouted tiny leaves like archetypes of emerald grandeur and the fruit trees bloomed in a riot of white and pink and on Crying Woman Ridge the petals of the wild plum trees from an abandoned orchard were banked like windblown snowdrifts. The new growth of leaves and mayapple softened the abrupt harsh angularity of the ridges and a warm wind looping up from the south set everything astir and gave the world the illusory quality of a mirage. Everything was blurred green motion.

Yates took heart. Since his daddy was killed, he was much in the woods, avoiding any place that the killer might be, sleeping wherever night fell on him, and he welcomed this moderation of the temperature. He saw this early spring as a gift from the fates. A balancing of some cosmic scale. The scent of wildflower rode the winds and he moved through this Edenic world with a newfound confidence. He began to think he might make it after all.

Later that year his mother told him she was going to die. She waxed and waned like a fever. She'd cough and cough by spells and chills would come on her and make her thin shoulders shake even when she was covered with quilts. She'd cough and spit bright bits of bloody spittle and the TB would burn in her cheeks in a dread illusion of health. She was going to die she said but he already knew everybody was going to die. She said he'd be sorry then and he guessed he would.

He was on the shady end of the porch waiting for cool dark to fall so he could be off when she pushed the screen door open.

I'm about out of that Chill Tonic, she said.

I ain't got none, he told her.

It was some kind of patent medicine she took. Some dark foulsmelling tonic. Even Yates knew it was worthless but he didn't begrudge her. He figured if you were dying you had coming most anything you wanted.

I know you ain't but Dow Cook's got a storeful. You go fetch me a bottle and tell him I said put it down on a ticket.

He won't.

Ask him anyhow, she said. Tell him I'll pay for it somehow.

Yeah, he said. Somehow is the way everything gets done around here.

Don't smartmouth me. Just do what I told you. It eases me.

All right, he said. I'll go directly.

I reckon you're restin, she said. She went back in and the door slapped to.

He sat on the porch awhile doing nothing and thinking no thoughts at all. Low in the west the sun flared red over a bright underpinning of goldlike latticework hammered from brass. Up Owl Hollow the crusher hammered like a foundry. He went in once and she was asleep in the rocker with her mouth open and he leant to see was she breathing.

It was far afterdark and whippoorwills calling when he came in. She was still asleep. It was very hot in the house and the air stale with doom as if death napped on the cot across the room. He got up and opened a window to the cries of nightbirds and the rich smell of honeysuckle. He lay back down and tried to sleep but it was still too hot.

For no reason he could name he thought of his father.

His father came in drunk one day with a baby goat. He never said where he got it or if he did Yates didn't remember. He figured he'd stolen it. Only his father would steal something as useless as a goat.

The baby goat was coal black with markings of white stockings and the boy named it Blackie. It grew to think of him as its master and it followed him as a dog might. It would come when he called it and nuzzle its soft hornless head against his face. Nights he kept the kid tied on a rope to keep dogs from killing it. He went out one morning and it had choked to death. It was wound up in the rope with its pink tongue distended, and unwinding the rope didn't help but when he released it, it toppled sideways and fell. He stood it up on the limber legs but it fell and he began to cry nor could he stop. He cried bitterly and brokenly as if awaiting someone to come console him but no one did.

At length he knew he had to bury it. There was no shovel. They did not even possess a shovel to bury the dead.

He was stubborn and sin came easily and early to him. He stole a shovel leant against the wall of the company store and when he came back into the glade his father was skinning the goat. His hands were bloody and he seemed to be flaying it. The boy knelt down, the shovel across his knees. He didn't say anything. Across the bloody kid his father's face was at once shamefaced and defiant. Then he looked away and wiped the bloody knife-blade on his pants and pocketed it. He threw aside the skin and arose, took up the kid by its legs and walked off.

After a time, Yates arose and shouldered the shovel and followed along behind. Yates's father turned up Owl Hollow and Yates had to hurry to keep up but after a time he decided he was going to Old Granny Stovall's and he didn't have to run so much.

When he came in sight of the bootlegger's, his father and the old woman were in the front yard talking. They seemed to be arguing about something. His father kept gesturing and pointing toward the goat, placating, and she kept shaking her head. Rows of old men in folding chairs on the porch watched like parishioners at some curious camp meeting. After a few minutes she seemed either to change her mind or become weary of the whole discussion. She threw up her arms disgustedly and then took a halfpint bottle from the back of her voluminous apron and gave it to him and he handed her the goat. She carried it at arm's length by one leg up the stairs then disappeared around back where the wraparound gave onto the rear porch. She came back into view without the goat and seated herself before the old men like some grotesque old queen preening before her court of degenerates.

The first thing his father did was uncork the whiskey and drink. The boy watched his Adam's apple work pumping the whiskey down. He wiped a sleeve across his mouth and put the bottle in the bib pocket of his overalls and straightened his shoulders, strolling off already staggering and listing like a sailor trodding an unsteady deck. The hangdog look was gone. In its place a subtle arrogance, an air of defiance, a man of the world who took nothing off of nobody as he was wont to say.

The boy watched from the brush. A sort of contempt touched him. Goin to go hang around the store till somebody kicks the livin shit out of you, he thought.

He eased around the hillside through a grove of scrub pine, the ground carpeted with old worn copper colored pine needles, the air heady with the astringency of the trees. No one seemed to know he was in the world. If they did, they didn't care. When the back porch came into view he could see the kid dangling from a short length of rope or wire. Halfway to the summit of the hill he stopped and began to dig. The ground was stony and full of roots but he worked steadily, using the shovel as a pry bar to free the stones, as a dull axe to cut through the roots. When he finally had what he figured was about goatsize he stopped and squatted to get his breath back. He was wet with sweat.

He dreaded this part. This part couldn't be done from the bushes. He watched the house. Fear that was almost terror knotted his stomach. Well, he said, somebody's got to do it and I guess it's me.

He'd thought the old woman still on the porch and he was surprised to see her coming around the corner of the house and into the edge of the pines as if she divined his presence or smelled his blood as childhood giants were told to do and he was holding his breath and making ready to flee when she looked all about and turned her back to him and hoisted her skirts. She squatted on the pine needles with her enormous pale hams turned nakedly up to him while she urinated and out of propriety or distaste he looked away until she was done.

An ugly child patterned on the fat woman came into the yard where a cluster of worn-out pans and broken dishes lay, a motley of broken and castoff appliances.

She selected a pan and filled it with alternating layers of dirt and buckeye leaves and set it on a makeshift stove to cook, all the while singing tunelessly to herself. An ugly girlchild curiously unchildlike. Some dread troll or dwarf in parodic and listless semblance of play.

Get away, you little slut, Yates thought. I've got a funeral to run here.

The troll went on humming and washing broken dishes in a pan of water and every once in a while she'd check the mess she'd concocted as if to see was it done, then she appeared to lose interest and wandered off trying to sneak up on a blueblack fighting cock that had wandered up out of the brush.

Yates was up and about the moment she was out of sight. He was soundless across the yard and fast up the wooden stairway and his hands were quick at the wire securing the kid. He had it up in his arms and was down the stairs and halfway to the pine thicket when the troll began to shriek. Mama, mama, it cried.

The woman was there instantly as if she'd been lying in wait for someone to steal her goat. You stop you goddamned little sneakthief, the woman cried.

Yates had no inclination toward stopping. There was something in the old woman's voice and something else in the troll's gleeful jumping up and down and shrieking that redoubled his efforts. He pumped his thin legs and tightened his spindly arms about the bloody thing and dove into the dwarf pines like a crazed but determined apprentice necromancer caught with what he had stolen flopping and slipping slickly away from his grip. He was running on adrenaline and stubbornness and sheer nerve.

He paused at the grave. He dropped the kid into it and took up the shovel as if he'd bury it and be damned in the very face of this firestorm of invective. But before he'd thrown the first shovelful of dirt the woman was lumbering toward him up through the brush. You turn aloose of my property, she was yelling, her fierce and diminutive familiar bringing up the rear. The old woman, a great shambling she-bear with slovening razorous teeth, set upon him with such murderous intent, a hot volatile smell of musk and anger and outrage. Coming through the brush she looked absolutely remorseless, the old she-bear with a cub in peril, or a territorial imperative.

It's mine anyway goddamn it, Yates cried, but the old red faced woman was laboring up the embankment breathing hard and hanging onto saplings to haul herself up. Her irongray hair had sprung out in disarray and her blue eyes were fierce and protuberant.

He hurled the shovel at her. He'd meant to behead her with its blade but the shovel turned in midair and only the handle slammed into the side of her head. The blow of the handle was relatively harmless but it was sufficient to make her release her grip on the sapling and when she did she plummeted downward like something caught in an instantaneous and horrific onset of gravity. She rolled on the troll, muffling momentarily the outraged shrieks as the two of them fell gracelessly end over end down the hillside. Yates scooped up the kid and was leaving with it when the two of them rolled to a halt in the pines. He could hear the crush of breaking branches and the whimpering of the troll and almost instantly the woman's voice.

I'll skin you, she shrieked. I'll skin you and hang you up, you little son of a bitch.

He didn't even answer. He was struggling down the summit with the goat and after a while he was on the old railroad bed going further than he'd ever been into the Harrikin and he couldn't hear her anymore.

Deep in the Harrikin before full dark fell on him he

came upon an enormous pile of steel rails wrecked out of the bed for scrapiron and beyond, a stack of halfrotten crossties. He began to pile brush about the tie pile and dead cedar stumps and all such tinder as he could find and, when he'd arranged it to his satisfaction, he laid the kid atop his makeshift pyre and set it afire.

It was the next afternoon when he got back home. Filthy and bloody and dazedlooking from wandering the Harrikin. First thing his father fell upon him with a strap but he didn't care. He'd been strapped before and would be again but such things pass.

What didn't pass was the look on his father's face when they faced each other across the bloody goat.

Trying to sleep in the whippoorwill dark he tried to call to mind something of comfort, something in all this darkness, some word of kindness, the weight of a gentle hand.

But his mind kept returning again and again to the same image. It was some wild animal, crouched above the wired goat like a predator interrupted at a meal halfeaten, its eyes bright with malice and its whiskers tinged with blood.

Allen's Creek Road ran east and west as did the railroad track, the creek itself. The summer morning sun cradled up out of the eastern hills directly over the point where the road faded into the timber, the red dusty road running straight as a chalked line into the sun as if some prior race with a penchant for astronomical accuracy had so aligned it. To his childhood eyes the sun shone only on

Allen's Creek, and beyond the point where it ascended in
the palest rose, and the point where it vanished in curdled
bloodred clouds at day's end, lay only trees, an infinity
of them, and darkness.

The world in each day's creation was ever pristine
and unused. The sun in its ascension rising above the
harsh green treeline imbued every living thing, every
twig and stone, with a surreal clarity. A marvelous other-
worldliness was yielding all things to all people, stark in
its simplicity, marvelous in its complexity as if no limits
had yet been erected. Each summer day lay before him
like a great undiscovered country, fecund and ripe, and
the possibilities were limited only by the scope of his
endurance, the limits of his imagination.

He used to just head out into it. It was already warm
as soon as the sun rose and he'd be off the porch and
gone, his mother shouting for him to come back, her
cries falling on deaf ears and there came some point he
wasn't even aware of when she stopped calling and he
was as free as an animal in the brush, a bird tilting on
the wing.

He'd drift through the greengold morning sun up
Gander Ridge, out onto the dry baked hardpan and into
the community of Allen's Creek, a community laid out
on no conceivable plan, a random scattering of houses
sprung up wherever necessity or convenience decreed,
a motley of perhaps a hundred houses ranging from
staid dignified farmhouses to the poorest shotgun shan-
ty, houses hauled in on a flatcar and nailed together as
Yates's own house had been. Folk drawn together with
no common objective save the removal of ore from the
earth.

A company store. A myriad of bootleggers. A post
office. Two permanent churches and a panoply of tents

and brush arbors were the esoteric home to footwashings, snakehandlers, poison drinkers. No school, no doctor, no undertakers, no law.

In time to come he'd look on all this with unscaled eyes.

Already the crusher was rumbling and downwind of it the air thick with dust. Ochrecolored dust, fine as graphite that clings to the trees, the earth, the folks themselves. Curious dust, folk like men imperfectly formed, as if creatures from a tale told from the earth itself. The dust thickly accumulates on vine and shrub and leaf, sealed and flaking when the dew had dried. When summer squalls blow in and the first slant sheets of rain fly, the trees run red as blood like the embodiment of some ancient Biblical plague.

At Dow Cook's store he sat midway up the tall front steps for a time with his hands laced about his knees doing nothing at all. The sun stood now at midmorning and its fierce July heat shimmered in the air so that the edges of things seemed to vibrate slightly. The trees stand numb and motionless in the breezeless air. An acrid spicy smell of hot weeds, sweet heady honeysuckle nectar. From a hollow still locked in sepia shade, a dove called its sad news, called again.

There was no one about. Everyone was at work. If it had been Saturday there would have been fights to watch but it wasn't Saturday. Saturdays he used to hide in an empty boxcar and watch. All day long there'd be fierce short explosions of violence when men drunk or men sober would pound each other into exhaustion and rest awhile and commence again like folk changing partners at some curious dance. Once through the slats of a boxcar he saw a man killed. Two men fought, then one of them pulled a knife. The other man fled. The man chased him up the red road brandishing the knife and swearing at him and they both turned up Paiton Hollow and vanished in the bracken. In a little while the pursuer came out alone. He folded the knife and dropped it into his overalls pocket. Almost an hour passed, and the incident seemed forgotten when the man came back out the Paiton Hollow road and when he did, he was carrying a shotgun breeched at port arms and striding purposely toward the high front porch.

Yates knew exactly what was going to happen. He was seized by utter and absolute terror, a cold fear the like of which he'd never known. He wanted desperately to be somewhere else, he wished he'd never come. He wanted to flee blindly as hard as he could and never look back but he was afraid the man would just shotgun him so he froze where he was and screamed as loud as he could.

Hey! he called.

The man who'd drawn the knife was leant against a Bruton snuff sign and he glanced uneasily about as if someone might step forward to avert this, but Yates was not the only one frozen. The air had turned somber and there was a dread inevitability to all this. He was holding a halfpint of white whiskey and he raised it in a gesture half placating and wore on his face a foolish tentative grin when the gun exploded, and his arm was blown away in a shower of glass and blood and whiskey. Yates saw the second barrel discharge and the man was simply jerked upward and back but he didn't see him land. He was up and running the moment the gun was empty and he leapt out the door and fled toward home.

Late in the day from his porch on Gander Ridge he saw a black turtlebacked car with a gold escutcheon on the door drive slow down toward the store and behind it, slow and stately and somber, a dusky black hearse. He was still there when they went back. He could see a dim figure in the back of the police car, but velvet drapes were drawn in the hearse and he couldn't see in at all.

All these acts of violence seemed random but already he divined something unseen moving beneath the surface, bones and blood and nerves beneath the skin.

He was sweating. He got up and went into the long hall-like building. It was cooler inside, darker, a fan whirred somewhere overhead. There was no one inside save Dow Cook behind the counter reading a newspaper through goldrimmed Pince-nez and a black man named Crowe whom Yates knew by sight, playing solitaire. He crossed to the dopebox and slid the lid back. Sodas stood shoulder to shoulder neck deep in ice water. He studied them. There seemed hundreds, thousands perhaps. Coca-Colas, Pepsi, orange and grape and strawberry Nehis, Pop Colas, Orange Crush in squat brown bottles. He felt in his jeans pockets as if he expected a miracle to have transpired. None had.

He stood before the counter. The storekeeper didn't look up. His lips moved, forming silent words.

How about stakin me to a Coca-Cola? Yates asked.

Dow looked up. I wouldn't stake you to the time of day, he said.

How about letting me sweep the floor then. I'd do it for a dope.

Dow went back to his paper. It don't need it, he said. I wouldn't sell you the time of day unless you paid me in advance.

Keep em then, Yates said.

He was halfway to the door when a voice stopped him. He turned. The black man was regarding him across the laid out cards. Come here a minute, he said.

Yates crossed the floor.

You want to do me a favor?

I don't know. I reckon so. What is it?

The black man's eyes were heavy lidded and sleepy-looking. His face was closed and impassive, it seemed to harbor secrets it dare not give away.

It's light easy work. I was wonderin if it was still hot outside. I thought maybe you might check for me.

Do what? Yates asked in disbelief.

It was a cold spell supposed to blow in here sometime today. Go see if it's got here yet.

Shit, Yates said. He'd fallen among mad folk here. He tried to read Crowe's face but there was nothing there to read. He couldn't tell if Crowe was making fun of him or if he was just naturally crazy. He turned and walked to the door and pushed the screen open and let it slap to behind him. Across the road the world shimmered in a whitehot haze. He's crazy as a shithouse mouse, he said aloud. He went back in.

It ain't cooled down none, he said.

Crowe nodded. About what I expected, he said. I'm much obliged to you.

He slapped a dime down on the table. Get yourself a dope, he said. Get yourself two.

Keep your money, Yates said. I ain't bummin one and I can't charge you for tellin you it's hot in the middle of July.

I had a job I wanted done and you done it to my satisfaction, Crowe said. A man is worthy of his hire.

I hate takin crazy folk's money, Yates said. But I reckon I will. He picked up the dime and pocketed it. He was already eyeing the dopebox. Let me know the next time you need a weather forecast.

A halfmile away from the store he was thirsty again and he left the road on a bare earth path padded out like the trail to an animal's den. He went under tendrils of honeysuckle and bright orange bells of cow itch through a steady droning of bees into a deep cloistered coolness with a damp reek of peppermint. The path abutted a bluff climbing steep, and sheer and a cold clear spring cascaded out of a fissure. Long ago someone had sledge hammered an iron pipe back into the crevices and water poured out into a springbox fashioned from enormous blocks of limestone. Yates knelt before it and drank deeply. The cold water distended his belly. He washed his face and slicked his hair back with the water and squatted for a time in the cold-spray, chewing a sprig of peppermint, studying the small lifeforms that dwelt in the limestone springbox where sand drifted as if curious winds blew down there in the cold deep, small crayfish ever retreating warily in the sandy depths. A bright orange spring lizard, tiny with black polka dots, its delicate humanlike fingers flexing nervously.

He arose and crossed the branch and went on downstream to where a steep rocky path began to climb the bluff, a wandering path that veered maddeningly back and forth, full of switchbacks around sharp turns laden with limbs of bush ivy. The old man's path worn mazelike into the earth. Stones themselves worn smooth by shoeleather, who knew how many trips, how many years.

Back from the bluff's summit the old man had hacked

back the thick undergrowth and fashioned a yard out of the forest and his shack set here. A temporary looking structure of poles and boards and blownoff tin replevied somewhere all roofed over with signs he'd come by over the years and lugged up the bluff. Advertisements for chill tonics and baking powders, cough syrups, nerve tonics and soft drinks, some no longer procurable. There was an arbor construed of fence wire strung between two poles and the old man's grapes were ripening, the fruit hanging in thick purple clusters, the air was full of their hot winy reek.

The old man was sitting on the shady side of the house the way Yates knew he'd be, in an old lounge chair with his packing crate of papers beside him. An old wooden orangecrate full of sheaves of manuscript pages, foolscap tablets, pokes, brown grocery sacks flattened and covered by the old man's nigh indecipherable microscopic scribbling, whatever fell to hand when inspiration was heavy on him.

Hey Mr. Mosier, Yates said. The wildhaired old man's white flowing beard seemed electrically charged by whatever current coursed his wiry frame, lighting up his fiercely blue maniacal eyes.

Young man, Mosier said gravely. Haven't seen you about for a while. Wife and children doing alright? This was the old man's idea of humor and Yates had heard it all before.

No more than just slippin by, Yates said. I hadn't checked on you in some time and I allowed you might have died. You still writin your Bible?

The old man gestured at his papers, a raised arm like a mad prophet. I'm still breathing, he said. I guess I'll kick out addressing the multitudes. I'm still working on it. Sometimes it seems an insurmountable task I've taken for myself.

I guess somebody had to do it.

I expect so. A thankless task right now but I expect recognition eventually.

You reckon it'll ever be a book? I mean a book like people read.

Why of course it'll be a book. If I live long enough to finish it. Why wouldn't it be a book? Every family will own one and I expect I'll be a very wealthy man. Not that I'm doing it for the money, you understand. As you mentioned yourself, someone had to do it. If a man could own a Bible that translated the Bible into language anyone could understand, with colloquialisms and so forth, don't you think every man would want one? Religion's greatest drawback has always been the obscurity of the scriptural text.

I reckon so, Yates said.

Go get yourself a cup of tea, Mosier said. The world is full of wickedness, but no more than this creek itself.

He knew Mosier would persist until he did, so he went in the back door. The old man's hovel was dark and cool and it smelled like nowhere Yates had ever been, a curious timeless smell of spices and roots and drying fruit and the old man's scuppernong wine working off in a five-gallon glass jar covered by a clean cloth, and the smell of the tea. The tea was in a pot on the cookstove. He selected a clean cup and poured, spooned in sugar and drank. Tea from the roots of a red sassafras tree the old man had dug, dark earthy taste of rootbeer in the back of his mouth. He went back out into the sun.

The old man was scribbling furiously again and perhaps he'd forgotten Yates. Yates seated himself in a castoff lawn chair and stared off across the yard. A sparrow was building a nest in an old sewing machine and Yates sipped his tea and watched it awhile. Nothing moved, not a tree, a leaf. Nothing save the sparrows in all that wilted world of July heat. When he turned back the old man was watching him.

You a reading man?

I can read. I don't have much call to. I been to school.

Folks are funny about reading, some of them. Ashamed of not being able to. I saw this fellow in the barbershop one time, I knowed him, he couldn't have read his name if a skywriter wrote it on the sky with an airplane. He was sitting there holding a newspaper pretending to read it. Moving his lips. Looking around to see if anybody was watchin him read that paper. Except he had it upside down. There was a picture of a big ocean liner on it and he was looking at it bottomside up and he said, 'Well I see where there's been a terrible shipwreck, lots of lives lost.'

I ain't that bad about it, to lie about it. I can read.

The old man proffered him a sheet of foolscap. See what you think of this, he said.

He supped his tea. He set his cup down and took the sheet and studied it a time with its curious quality of transparency.

This is from Exodus, the old man said. Moses has received the ten commandments and has come down the mountain.

Most of it just looked like henscratches to Yates but one sentence fairly leapt out at him.

You sinful shitasses, Moses screamed at the cavorting multitudes.

He shook his head and handed the sheet back.

The old man was regarding him quizzically. You have some objection? A literary critic are you?

I don't know, Yates said.

The word cavorting. I was dubious about that myself.

I don't know, Yates said again. Somehow I don't think Moses would have called all them folks shitasses.

Why not?

He thought awhile. It just don't sound like the way Bible folks ort to talk, he said. Him a Bible bigshot and all. You'd think he'd be above it.

Ahh. The very essence of what I'm doing. I'm taking the Bible out of the hands of the bigshots, as you call them, and giving it back to the ordinary man. Reducing it to common language.

Calling a bunch of Bible folks shitasses is pretty common, all right.

Don't you think he was angry? Don't you think God himself was angry? He caused them to wander in the wilderness for forty years. He'd have called them shitasses himself.

Looks like you'd be afraid of a lightning bolt right out of the sky or God could stop your heart and not even break a sweat.

Let him. I'm an old man ninety years old and weary to the bone. It'd take this awesome task off my shoulders and I'd get a little rest.

You'd get a lot of rest, Yates said. He got up to go and the old man solicitously accompanied him to the edge of the glen, but his heart wasn't in it. He was carrying his tablet along and he kept glancing at it.

Go on and get back to your work, Yates said.

You come back and see me, the old man said. Seems like a little company sort of sets me up sometimes. Sharpens me up to work. I aim to tackle Revelations when I finish this. I can't wait to wade in on that.

At the spring Yates stopped and drank cold water again and sat for a time on a stone in the shade pondering.

He couldn't figure the old man. Was he crazy? Did

he really think he was writing a Bible? Or was he just doing it for his own amusement, whittling away at time that
lay heavy on an old man's hands? A new thought occurred
to him. The old man had written about Moses while he
was getting the tea and shown it to him for a joke. It was
the old man's idea of humor.

It was too much for him. Finally, he wrote the old
man off as crazy and got up and went on.

Dow Cook had come by a glass jeweler's case somewhere and it set by the window in his store. It was framed
with black steel and shelved with plate glass. It was filled
with oddments of dusty bric-a-brac and harmonicas and
Jew's harps and dollar pocketwatches and knives.

On the second shelf, resting just where the light from
the windows struck it was a knife the boy used to come
in and stare at. The knife lay in its box on a bed of cotton.
It was open. It had smooth wooden handles of walnut or
rosewood and etched on the blade was the likeness of a
stag's head. Below the stag it said: *White Face Cutlery
Inc*. Inset in the wood was a metal circle framing the pew-
ter stag.

Every time he came in Yates went straight for the
jeweler's case. He wanted that knife. He wanted it the
way a thirsty man wants water, a drowning man wants air.
His greatest fear was that someone would buy it before he
got the money. But the knife was four dollars and that was
a lot of money and so far had been passed over.

This day when he came in there was an air of purpose about him. He just gave the case a cursory glance to

ensure the knife was still there and strode to the counter where Dow was.

I want that knife, he said.

Dow was sitting on a barstool behind the counter. He had cheese and crackers before him on white butcher paper and he was eating his midday meal. He didn't even get up.

He chewed and swallowed and wiped cracker crumbs off his mouth. Well that's good, he said. You want it and I want to sell it. When you get the four dollars then we'll both be happy.

Yates laid four quarters on the counter, arranged them in a neat stack. I been thinkin, he said. I want to put that knife on layaway. I'll give you a dollar and you keep the knife. I'll come in along and pay on it and you keep the knife. After awhile I'll have it paid off. What about that?

The black man everyone called Black Crowe was leaning against the counter drinking a Coca-Cola. He opened a package of peanuts and dumped them into the bottle. The Coke foamed up and he drank the foam and stood, chewing peanuts and listening bemusedly and watching this exchange.

Dow Cook was shaking his head. I can't do it, he said.

Can't do it? Hellfire. Why can't you do it?

Don't cuss me, boy. I'm liable to rattle them jaws. I'll tell you why I can't do it. Say you pay me a dollar on it. Another feller comes in tomorrow and wants to buy it for four. Well, it's tied up. I can't sell it. Say you never come back and pay no more and I'm stuck with the knife. I've made a dollar and lost four. That's bad business.

Get another knife, the black man said.

Dow gave him a sharp glance. Do what? he asked.

I doubt that company made one knife like that and

then quit. You could take his dollar. Hold the knife like he said and order another one tomorrow for this feller with the four dollars. You could get another knife.

I could run my business to suit myself, Dow said, and that's just what I aim to do. Nobody asked you anyway.

Crowe set the Coke bottle down. Let me see this famous knife everybody's fighting to buy, he said. He started toward the jeweler's case.

There were a halfdozen idlers lounging about the store though it was long past the cold days of winter and not a breath of air stirring. From long habit they were grouped about the unlit heating stove. A gambler named Swain was dealing himself poker hands on an overturned Coke crate. He looked up sharply as Crowe went by. I wouldn't butt in Cook's business, he said.

Crowe didn't even look at him. Dow works for the public, he said. I'm part of the public. His business is my business.

He took the knife from the case and went back to the counter. He tilted the knife to the light and studied it, tried the blade on the hair on his arm. Yates was watching him. It's a good knife, Crowe said.

You damn right it's a good knife, Dow said. You buyin it or what?

It's a good knife but it ain't four dollars good. I seen one just like it in Ackerman's Field for three.

Then buy you one in Ackerman's Field, Dow said. I don't have to sell it to niggers anyway or him neither for that matter. You both just wastin my time.

Crowe was fumbling in his shirt pocket. He carefully counted three worn one dollar bills on the countertop, rubbing each with his fingers to ensure none were stuck together. Here, he said. I'll pay you for the knife and the boy can pay me whenever he wants to. That suit you?

It might if there was one more dollar bill lyin there.

Let's say it was marked a dollar off. You makin your profit all right. You don't have to make everything off one halfgrown boy.

Quietly Swain had pocketed his cards and arisen from the Coke crate and approached the counter. Watching them both the boy saw that Crowe was aware of it and was watching Swain out of the tail of his eye. Yates had heard neither the creaking of the Coke crate nor Swain's steps on the plank floor.

Crowe just stood holding the knife. There was a deceptive indolence about him. He looked calm and placid and, trying to read his expression, the boy found nothing there at all.

Dow had made no move to pick up the money. I can't do it, he said.

It's done already, Crowe said. I've paid you. You can pick it up or leave it lay.

Crowe, Swain asked, why in hell are you buttin into this. If the kid ain't got the money to pay for the knife, then that's the end to it.

I don't have to explain my motives any more than you do. I never asked you why you was buttin in.

I want my knife, Dow said. It's my goddamned store and if I say it's a four dollar knife then it's a four dollar knife. You keep the knife you ain't doin nothin but stealin it.

Crowe looked at him. Then count the losses, he said.

Dow opened his mouth to speak and then he looked at Crowe's face and he did not. For a moment he had looked into Crowe's eyes and what he saw there gave him pause. Crowe looked like a man who did not care one way or the other, who had been off the rim of the earth into hell and done everything and was perfectly willing to go again if only he could bring two or three along for company. Dow looked through the eyes to some barren and fireravaged landscape of eternal cold winds and it was a place he did not want to go to. Almost as if his right hand existed independent of him and possessed a will of its own it crept across the counter and took up the money.

Dow, are you letting this nigger buffalo you? It was me I'd slap him silly and take my knife.

Crowe turned to him. He held the knife clasped loosely. He didn't say anything.

I might have a pistol in my pocket. A knife ain't much against a pistol.

Have you?

Do what?

Have you got a pistol in your pocket?

An angry flush crept past Swain's white shirtcollar and suffused his face. Against his livid cheeks a long tapering scar stayed the pale sick yellow of dead flesh.

No, he said.

Crowe nodded. A made up pistol then. An imaginary pistol. A real knife against a made up pistol is a whole other thing.

Swain swallowed visibly.

I could give this boy his knife and then we'd be even.

He closed the blade and reached the knife to Yates but his eyes didn't move off Swain.

You better watch your back, he finally said.

I've done it so long its second nature to me now, Crowe said. Take your knife and go home, boy.

Yates was halfway to the door when he remembered the quarters. He went back to the counter and slid them toward Dow. Here, he said. This makes it even. This makes four dollars and it don't have to be no trouble.

The storekeeper didn't answer. He raked the coins

with his left hand into the palm of his right. His hands shook slightly. He wouldn't meet Yates's eyes.

Swain disappeared from Allen's Creek for a few weeks. Loungers at Dow Cook's store figured he didn't want to show his face and was laying low till the altercation was forgotten.

He'll be here before payday with his cards and dick, one of them said. Fools and paydays is the two things that Swain can't resist.

Swain was indeed back on payday. Yates watched from inside the store as Swain gave every man lounging on the store's high front porch a halfpint of whiskey. The old ones were somewhat taken aback by this unaccustomed generosity, but they accepted the whiskey anyway. Much obliged, they said. They sat and drank solemnly and waited for the check to arrive, the other shoe to fall.

Finally, it did. We fixin to teach that nigger a lesson tonight, Swain said. We're not fixin to put up with a nigger talkin to white men the way he does.

Nobody answered him.

We'll beat the hell out of him and point him out of here.

A man named Breece stoppered the bottle and slid it into the side pocket of his overalls. A man goes through another man's door in the middle of the night a askin for a faceful of shot, he said. Whatever color he might be.

Others nodded. Without speaking to each other they seemed to be of the same mind. It was true black was black and white was white, but they didn't like Swain.

Swain did not work save haulin bootleg whiskey and
taking money with the turn of a card, and the shrewdest
among them knew Swain was not averse to creasing the
cards. Pricking them with a straightpin. They had an in-
grained distrust of anyone who did no work. There's carpenters and there's lowdown mean sons of bitches. The
carpenter gets up on Monday morning and goes to work.
Swain gets up on Monday morning and goes to work bein
a mean son of a bitch. Swain's job carries its own respon-
sibilities, he has his own standards to live up to, rules, like
anything else. It was how he made his living and he was
working overtime. To him it was a matter of principle.
Everyone knew Dow kept his stock of groceries marked
fifteen or twenty percent higher than what they could be
bought for in Ackerman's Field but few people on Allen's
Creek owned cars and it was a long walk back to Ackerman's Field.

Hellfire, Swain said. He ain't but one man. He can't
shoot everybody.

Breece laughed mirthlessly. He can shoot the first
two or three through the door. If you can find two or three
to kind of lead the way and distract him and draw his attention. I might bring up the rear.

Swain looked at them. They met his gaze flaccidly
and these were rough old boys who were not averse to
going through doors unannounced, but he could see they
weren't going to help him.

Ever goddamned one of you is chickenshit right to
the bone, Swain said. I'll get him my damn self.

Breece nodded. That might be best, he said, seein as
how you've had more experience at it than the rest of us.

Swain didn't answer. He sat a few moments longer
and then he got up and smoothed the creases carefully
back into his slacks and crossed the porch to the steps

and went down. After a time Yates heard the Ford crank. Swain gunned the motor a few times and drove away.

With the sun warm on his back and a balmy wind looping up out of the riverbottom hollow, Yates came down the manmade mountain of rocks leaping stone to stone, a wary eye out for copperheads that want to den in the rocks. He could feel the rabbits jarring about inside his buttonedup shirt, crawling around his waistline, the unaccustomed almost unimaginable softness of their fur, once in a while the tickling from an ear. Their cool noses nuzzling him.

The mountain of rock from the washer tended gradually out into a wide bottomland between two tiers of bluffs. A logroad wound through it and crossed the Paiton Hollow road and in the clearing at the crossroads he halted.

All there was of sound was the running of waters and birds calling from off somewhere in the trees. It was Sunday and the crusher and the washer were silent. Then faroff and faint he could hear singing from the church on the main road, dreamlike, a distant chorus inquiring was he washed in the blood of the lamb.

One by one he took out the baby rabbits and aligned them on the grass. Four of them. He examined them closely, a finger tracing the delicate curvature of an ear, the intricate delicate craftsmanship of the nostrils. You couldn't devise anything so complex. A schoolteacher couldn't, the smartest man in the world couldn't. Immediately they began to stealthily crawl away. He brought them back and, clasped so in his hand, he could feel life hammering desperately inside them.

You alright now, he told them. The dog's gone. I saved your life and you belong to me now. You got to do what I say.

He'd found them in a sagegrass nest in a patch of blackberry briars, and he'd practically had to fistfight Abner Brewer's yellow hounddog for possession of them. It had taken a goodsized rock in the dog's slatted ribs to dissuade him and then he'd just retreated a few feet and sat watching Yates surlily.

He gathered up his rabbits and restored them to his shirt, turned and went on up the Paiton Hollow fork. The road narrowed as the hollow deepened and he was soon walking between nighvertical hills, enormous beeches clung to the walls in defiance of gravity and their branches bowered the road so heavily that now he moved in total shade, looking up there were only random arrows of green light falling plumb through the trees. Paiton was a dark hollow, night fell here sudden as a thunderclap, owls and doves called all day long from the shadowed sidehollows.

Where the road turned into a footpath and the hollow headed out there was a gray house set in the lee of the hills. A loghouse with two big rooms and a dogtrot between. Along the clapboard side of the house some long ago wit had painted *MULEDICK SALOON* in enormous letters. The red barn paint had run and dripped like blood and eventually faded a pastel pink. A high porch ran the full width of the house and usually there'd be folks sitting about he could tell about the rabbits but today there was no one. All the usual drunks and highrolling one penny ante poker players seemed struck alike by some Sunday constraint that kept them away from the Muledick.

He went down the path to the spring. The air was winy with peppermint. A tin cup hung on a cutoff stob. He took it down and rinsed it and drank. The water was very cold. A oneclaw crayfish retreated beneath a rock, white sand arose and stirred in the current and slowly settled.

What do you think you're doin?

He looked up. Lillie Mae Stovall was watching him from the edge of the wood. Lillie Mae was a big girl, four or five years older, grown or what passed for it in these provinces. She had fierce little bestial eyes and her broad face wore a perpetual look of suspicion, as if the world was constantly trying to put one over on her and she wasn't about to put up with it.

Mindin my own business.

Mind it somewhere else.

Yeah. I reckon you got the deed to Paiton Holler in your back pocket. I got as much right here as you have. Maybe more. What's a girl doin hangin around the Muledick?

I was supposed to meet somebody here.

If he's got any sense he won't show up. You seen Crowe around anywhere?

I ain't studyin that crazy nigger. I got bigger fish to fry. Everbody's gone. Crowe wadn't here anyway. Brewer's down drunk and threatenin to kill everbody and won't tell where his whiskey's hid. They all piled in Swain's car and went somewhere.

Swain? Mean lookin feller drivin a black Ford jacked up in the backend? Got a knife scar down his jaw?

That's him all right. He's some kind of a highroller.

He felt a soft furtive movement against his ribcage and held a protective arm to try to hide the movement, but she saw it anyway, her beady little eyes saw everything.

What've you got in there?

Nothin.

What're you hidin in your shirt? You don't tell me

I'll get you down and pull off your britches and spit on your little thing.

He studied her as if measuring her, mentally weighing her. She looked capable of it.

Reluctantly he took out the rabbits one by one and laid them in the leaves.

Aww, she said. She approached them, touched one with a hand he wouldn't have expected to be so gentle. Ain't they sweet?

Something in her voice drew his eyes to her face. Some strange note of tenderness, a maternal tone he wouldn't have thought her capable of.

I want em, she said. This time there was just finality in her voice.

Well you can't have em. Hellfire. Get your own rabbits. These is mine.

What'll you take?

They ain't for sale. You'd just kill em anyway to watch em die.

I might. Then again, I might not. Maybe I just want somethin of mine, that belongs to me. Look. I'll trade you for em.

You ain't got nothing I want.

She glanced all about the woods. She lowered her voice, although there seemed no one around for miles.

I'll let you do what the big boys do.

Do what?

You give me them rabbits and I'll show it to you. I'll let you do it to me.

Right here?

Sure, right here. Ain't nobody around and the leaves is soft. You want to?

I don't know, he said. His voice sounded strange. He glanced around. There was no one. He'd half hoped there would be. He seemed to be at the borders of the region that was foreign to him.

Show it to me.

She raised her shirt about her waist and hooked her thumbs in the top of her drawers and pulled them down.

There, she said. There was a curious sense of power in her voice. I bet you ain't never seen nothing like that. I bet you ain't never even seen one with hair on it before.

He leant closer, the better to study this morsel. I never seen one with sourgnats around it like that neither.

Well, come on. Let's see if you can do it. You want to swap?

He was looking all around, studying avenues of escape. He'd begun to gather up his rabbits, stuffing them carefully back into his shirt.

I got to get on, he said.

Why goddamn you. You lyin little shitass. I showed it to you and at least one of them rabbits is mine. I know what your trouble is. You can't do it. You can't even make it hard. You just chickenshit.

No, I ain't. I just rather have my rabbits.

She was standing there crazily threatening him with her underwear to her knees. Then she hauled them up and started across the branch toward him, and for a moment they feigned across the brook in a drunken ballet. Then she lunged toward him and, clutching the rabbits, he ducked under an outstretched arm and was gone into the trees. She ran a few steps after him, but he was fairly flying toward the mouth of the hollow.

You'll pay for this, she yelled after him.

He went down by the side of the bluff to check on his rabbits. He had them in the bottom of a caved-in cistern and he hunkered on the edge and peered down. There was only one left. It looked none too healthy. He'd fed them lettuce and wild grasses but, all the same, one by one, they fell sick and one by one they died. He'd climbed down the stony throat of the cistern and retrieved them and buried them until he'd begun to feel like a diminutive but conscientious undertaker.

Don't you die, he told it. And I mean it.

It didn't say if it would or it wouldn't. It just watched him with its little glass eyes.

I'm fixin to get you a cabbage head or somethin, he said. You wait here a minute.

Old Mrs. Springer was in her garden with a hoe and beneath the trim of her bonnet her bright little eyes dared him into the garden. He couldn't find any cabbage but came back with a handful of wild lettuce and threw it into the cistern. The rabbit didn't pay any mind. It lay on its side with its shoebutton eyes looking at nothing, but it wasn't dead for its thin sides pumped like gills.

I meant what I said, he told it.

He went back out to check on the rabbit before dark and it was dead. It lay on its side with its eyes open and ants crawled over its face. Die then goddamn you, he told it. He tried to cry. He gave a dry sob or two but he couldn't seem to work up any tears and he soon gave it up. He wandered off toward the mines. He felt as if he'd been always burying them and throwing dirt on them and seeing them no more.

Of a morning, before good light with fog pale as milk marking the creek below the trestle, they'd fall out, all of a good heart, a loose unfocused mob of them at the mouth of Owl Hollow. A line of teams and wagons strung out back up the road; if you owned a team and wagon and wanted to use it hauling ore you drew a salary for yourself and a salary for the team. If all you had to sell was the labor of your own body you clustered with these gaunteyed men clutching their lunchbuckets waiting for the work whistle to blow.

To the side and standing apart from all this rough camaraderie, even from the company of each other, were always a half dozen and oftimes substantially more men standing there in the halfdark smoking silently and just waiting on the off chance some man didn't show up. Drunk, in jail, knifecut. You laid out of work here at your own peril, for if you laid down your job, there was always another pair of hands already reaching for it. Bitter times and a seller's market and whatever the strawboss said you just took and went on.

Anybody seen Clyde? Albert Paiton wanted to know. Nobody wanted to tell him anything. Some of these men felt Paiton didn't have to work and he was just taking up a job some other man needed.

Nobody ain't seen Clyde, he said aloud to himself.

I ain't got no helper, he told the boss.

Then get a helper, the foreman said. All these warm bodies. Clyde ain't the only man in the world can help charge a hole.

I'll go, a faceless man called from the sidelines.

I need somebody knows what he's doing, Paiton

said, searching the sea of faces, settled finally on no face but Crowe's. Perhaps darker than the rest, Crowe's own face sought him out and later Crowe spent time trying to figure what drew Paiton's eyes to his own.

I'll take old Black Crowe, he said.

Crowe never showed surprise but now he came as close as he had ever come. He knew Paiton didn't like him.

Me?

Less you'd rather run a sledgehammer, Paiton said.

I wouldn't mind havin a job with all the work done picked out of it, a man said.

I want Crowe.

What the hell, Crowe said. I can stand an easy day for a change.

These were rootless days of comings and goings un-announced or remarked upon and Clyde was just gone. Perhaps he'd won a lottery, been sent to prison, buried in a shallow grave. Clyde was just not there anymore and for three days Crowe labored at his job.

Crowe had to work with Albert Paiton, but he didn't like it.

Albert Paiton was socially a cut above the payday-to-payday folks he worked the mines with. His overalls were always clean and his chambray shirts freshly laundered. He chewed Sen-Sen for his breath and always smelled of it. His face seemed always just shaved and talcumed. He owned his own farm and he and his wife raised cattle and sold milk and butter. Possibly he would not have had to work there at all, or if he'd had to swing a pick and shovel, he wouldn't. But Paiton was a powder man, and there was a certain superiority about this.

Paiton was not very well liked. He had a sly, knowing way of looking at people they didn't take to. He seemed to know things that you didn't, or things only you knew about yourself. God seemed to have taken him aside conspiratorially, leant and whispered secrets in his ear the rest of the world wasn't privy to yet. He'd look you in the eyes as if you and he almost shared some secret, you just weren't in on it.

They also didn't trust him. He laid the charges offhand, careless. That sweet smellin son of a bitch is goin to blow somebody skyhigh, they said.

Secretly Crowe thought Paiton wanted to die. Or if he didn't actually seek death at least he was passive about it, he didn't mind dying. Just whatever come along. He'd load the charges too heavy. He'd use too short a fuse. He'd light the fuse and laugh and they'd have to crawfish madly back down off the bluff with Paiton laughing crazily and Crowe swearing and trying to protect himself from imminent flying rock, looking for something to get behind. With fear bordering on panic, he could feel the explosion fanning outward from the pit of his stomach while he was scrambling over outcroppings of limestone that would not even be there a few seconds from now.

The day they blew the Owl Hollow bluff it was windy, a spring storm in the air. They had to fan out on the bluff to pack the charge. Crowe wondered how much the bluff had been weakened by the drilling. It seemed to hang there, defying gravity. Let's go Black Crowe, Paiton said. You want to live forever?

You better give us time to get back off this bluff. You cut this fuse short and I swear I'll cut your throat, Crowe told him. White man or not.

You don't like bein a powderman. I'll see about gettin you a pick and shovel. Paiton looked up from the bore
he was packing with black powder. He grinned. His yel-
lowed teeth clutched a pipestem, and Crowe was suffused
with horror. Paiton puffed the pipe mockingly and Crowe
could smell the blue tobacco smoke. In the moment Paiton winked in an almost surreal way, Crowe noticed that
his eyelid was lashless, there was something birdlike or
reptilian about it, just a pouched flap of flesh that closed
and opened obscenely off and on. For the rest of his life
Crowe pondered that wink, what it meant. Did it mean
Don't worry, I got this charge all under control, everything's going to work out all right? There was something
complicit in it: did he know the bluff was going up instantly and share this knowledge only with Crowe, did
he know already what the men out of harm's way and
watching would see moments later?

Leant over the powder and still tamping it with his
hand, Crowe opened his mouth to speak. He said something but the wind got it. The wind twisted the pipe in
Paiton's grinning mouth and the coal of burning tobacco
tipped out and they simply were not there anymore.

Instantly there was a wall of noise so dense you could
touch it, an onset of rushing black wind that seized him
and bore Crowe and what there was of Paiton upward in a
concussion of black smoke and chunks of earth and rock,
weightless, not only weightless but all alike possessed of
a kind of antiweight that flung them freefalling toward a
bright blue void that Crowe could still see through a veil
of fire and powdered rock. Then it was momentarily dark
and the sun vanished and he could see the pinprick light
of stars and a dead moon tracking palely westward. He
turned and arced in a foiled and graceless dive through the

popping and snapping of pine branches and was abruptly halted upside down, constrained he hung suspended, his flight halted by a searing pain down the length of his right leg.

When he came to men were getting him down out of the shattered tree. There was an enormous rushing in his ears. The water, he said, clasping his ears hard with his palms to shut out the sea. His hand came away bloody. The earth they laid him on was alien to him, a field of splintered stone and broken tree branches and shifting haze of dust, a land out of a fever dream. The colors were not right, objects stood out in bold dark relief. The men's faces were pale and strained, their lips gibbered at him but said no word he could hear. They laid him on his back on the rocks and the blue sky looked far, far away. He'd rest here awhile then drift on into it. Far above him a haze of rockpowder and smoke still shifted and farflung pieces of rock and of Paiton were falling like the last bitter blackened rotten fruit of autumn the wind gets. He thought of the bluff almost superstitiously as if, had the earth here been less barren, everywhere a chunk of Paiton fell like a malign seed another Paiton would grow.

Crowe was young then, perhaps only thirty-five, but still, he was a long time healing, and after that day he was a middleaged man. A broken tree branch hooked into the fleshy part of his upper thigh and ripped to the calf. He couldn't hear out of his left ear, there was only a soft faroff murmur that sounded like distant voices, timbre and cadences, the words indecipherable, and he'd perpetually turn his head slightly to rightward to understand you. For a while folks thought he would die but he would not. His leg slowly healed into a long spurling scar that wound the length around his leg. For a long time he didn't walk at all. He lay on his cot that summer with the hot sun baking the tin roof while his flesh warred with gangrene, soaking in blood and sweat and corruption.

He lay sweatsoaked facing the windows where at night summer storms flared and died and the wind sang rain off the tin and Paiton's sly face swam in his mind like a vision. Reality came and went, and these were times when he thought Paiton was still alive and the only thing that allayed the pain was the thought of cutting his throat. The straightrazor sliding through flesh was a temporary delusion but the pain was a constant. This pain even had a color, a dull burnished red, the color of coke burning in the brick furnaces he'd stoked as a boy, a hot red that ebbed and throbbed but would not subside.

A few people from the mines came once or twice then no more. He was poor company. Crowe was in no mood for small talk and they could only sit awkwardly on the odd canebottom chair while Crowe lay there silent with his eyes closed but somehow not there, off in an alien world of his own where the only reality he accepted was pain. After a while they'd say they had to get on. Except for the Yates boy. The Yates boy and the old widow bootlegger from the Muledick who said, I never was much of one for niggers but I'd not let a dog starve to death. She brought soup when he couldn't cook. When he began to mend the woman quit coming. The boy came every day. He brought fresh water from the spring and he'd wordlessly hand Crowe a cool dipper from the cedar bucket.

He didn't say much. He sat in the silence the room was steeped in. The room seemed some warehouse where time was stored. Even the calendars marked years long past. He'd sit with his back against the wall and his arms looped about his knees watching Crowe as if he didn't have any other place to be or another thing in all the world to do till Crowe needed tobacco from the store or a fire built in the cookstove to make coffee. He whittled a walking stick from a hickory sapling so entwined with honeysuckle vines that a spiral groove wound its length. Into the wood he cut crescent moons and stars and strange hieroglyphs that held no meaning beyond his carving of them. For all his faults he was a good provider. He was that, Crowe agreed. He provided me a damn sight more than I wanted.

Boy if you lookin for work I ain't hirin, he said, and even if I was I got no money to pay you.

I don't need no money. I got money of my own.

Then what are you doin here.

Well. Hell. I don't see you totin water from the spring. I reckon you want a smoke whether you say so or not. Ain't that right?

I reckon so, Crowe finally said.

Then there you are.

It was said Crowe read books. It was even said that in his youth he had been a teacher at a black school in rural Maury County and perhaps he had. At any rate, he had what for Allen's Creek was a curious way of talking. He said, Boy what did I ever do to earn your undyin gratitude.

The boy was silent a time. You don't know how bad I wanted that knife.

Yeah, I do. That's why you got it.

I never seen anything like that. You just sort of took it.

No, I never. I paid what it was worth. If my price and his didn't agree then toughshit.

Anyway, I wanted it.

Sure you did and it was something I could do that didn't cost me much. If I could go through the world givin everbody whatever they want the most, I'd do it. But the world don't work that way. Everbody won't settle for a four-dollar knife.

Well I did. And you can say what you want to but it won't change me havin the knife. What would you have done if he'd called you on it? Swain, I mean.

Crowe halfsmiled. He's a baldheaded old man with a gut, he said. I been to places it's hard to come back from. What would he do to me?

There is nothing that is a thing to itself, Crowe told him. No event that stands alone, separate from all other events. Everything that happens is influenced by what came before and it in its turn influences what comes after.

I reckon so, Yates said agreeably. He was leant against the wall of Crowe's shack listening to Crowe talk and watching Crowe drink whiskey.

He'd gone to the Muledick himself for the bottle. Medicine, Crowe had said. When he sipped on a whiskey awhile the ache in his leg was easier to bear.

Crowe was sitting in the rocker before the fire with the bad leg outstretched for the heat, taking from time to time a sip of the clear bootleg. On his lap was the worn double F guitar but he made no move to play it save the occasional inadvertent brushing of the strings. He seemed to draw a curious comfort from just holding it.

Yates liked to hear him talk. Half the time he didn't know what he was talking about, but he liked hearing him anyway. There was a strange comfortable kinship between them, Crowe and the whiskey and the fire and the night beyond the walls. He had noticed long ago that there was more than one Crowe and that each Crowe had a different way of talking. The Crowe at Dow's or the Muledick or the mines talked like everybody else. The Crowe that Yates knew talked like a schoolteacher, like a voice in the radio, that sometimes drank whiskey and talked to Yates far into the night.

Crowe was part black and part Indian and he didn't know what else. Whatever was left, Crowe ended up with whatever nobody else wanted. Crowe figured back in the beginning of time, God mixed life up in some kind of a beaker and began pouring folks out and it was hard work. After awhile he got tired and took a break or maybe lit up a smoke and when he again took up the beaker of life, the dark and undesirable and insoluble dregs had settled at the bottom where they grew into a malignancy and, when he poured him out, that was Crowe.

Events arrange themselves in a series, Crowe said. Stack themselves, if you prefer. Arrange them. Events make a life. Give it a symmetry. Like all lives, my life was a segmented series of events and, like all other lives, it was a delicate thing that could be uncoupled by one event throwing things out of balance. Everything can fall down. My life fell down.

He drank from the bottle, held it against the firelight as if to gauge how much remained. His voice was always mellifluous and unslurred by the liquor.

The particular event that was my own undoing was the death of a child, Crowe went on. The child was my own, and I killed him with my own hand, with an axe that I carried into the wood. And when that toppled, all things toppled and it was not a life that I knew anymore.

Yates didn't know if Crowe was lying or not. He never knew. There was an aura of truth about everything that he said or did, but at the same time there was an undercurrent faintly mocking that seemed to want to show

how big a fool he could make out of you.

There was a time when my life had an awesome symmetry, Crowe said. I had a wife. I had a child. I had a job that earned me the respect of every man I knew. I was a schoolteacher.

How did you ever get to be a schoolteacher?

Crowe drank. A white man took an interest in me, he said. My people were sharecroppers. Generations before that they were slaves. There's not much difference between the two except that white people sharecrop too. Slavery is more exclusive. Anyway, this man my father cropped for took an interest in me. He was not a cruel man or a particularly kind man. I suppose I was a curiosity to him, for I could read before I was three years old. This in a time when few black folks read at all. This man was a country lawyer and one time he was sipping his juleps on the porch and, as I polished his boots, he taught me to talk like a white man. I found that wasn't a particularly desirable thing and that I didn't fit. I wasn't like the people who had raised me and I wasn't like the people I had been trained to be. I was somewhere in between. Sometimes closer to one than the other but never completely in either. I could see too many sides of the same question.

There was a young girl from Chapel Hill who was foolish enough to fall in love with me. We married and she bore me a son. One day when he was eight years old, I went into the woods to cut a tree for firewood. He followed me into the woods slipping along behind me and watching me like it was a joke. It was no joke when I cut a tree and on this still day, a gust of wind arose and the tree broke at the stump and fell the opposite way and landed right on top of the boy and I couldn't push it off of him. If I had known that was death reaching out to grasp his hand

— he stopped and lit the cigarette. By the glow of the match his face was orangeblack and gleaming and there was no look there at all. No grief, no regrets, as if the face were some material other than the flesh and bone, that it had transcended and was incompatible to life's weathers. Yates couldn't see his eyes. Dark holes like eyeholes in death's head.

Do you understand the significance of what I said? A wind arose from nothing. There was no wind and, from nothing, a wind twisted the tree backward off the stump and crushed him impersonally like a flyswatter crushes a fly. I had to go back to the house. There were no words to explain it to her, but she had a God to turn to. To her he was in heaven playing on streets of gold. To me, he was just irrevocably in the ground. Here I was, an educated negro with a kinship to Kierkegaard. Life had stalemated for me. Death is crawling through a narrow stone passageway where sharp and dangerous edges are padded by quilted satin stolen from the undertaker's lair. Echoing life you move blindly forward and on the graven stone you crawl on your fingertips, read the names of those who've gone before until the chasm opens abruptly into an enormous room without walls, ceiling or floor, utterly dark, profoundly silent. I was on death's doorstep with a finger on the doorbell.

One day, I walked into the kitchen because I heard her laughing eerily. She didn't hear me and I opened my mouth to speak. Of a sudden glass broke behind me and a perfect hole appeared in the hollow of her throat. Her eyes seemed to glaze before she hit the floor. Only then did I hear the shot. I never did find out what she was laughing about.

He fell silent again. This time there was an air of finality about it. He drank from the bottle and put it carefully behind his foot. He sat composed and silent, his eyes closed. He seemed to have no plans to ever speak again.

What did you do?

I did what I had to do, Crowe said. What any man has to do. When you've been where I had been, seen what I had seen, you can do whatever it is you have to do to survive.

Swinging the bucket along in his hand, he crossed purposefully through a stand of wild cane and, without stopping or even slowing, went on into the creek, the water thighdeep here and cold even in the summer heat. A moment before, he was wet with sweat but he shivered involuntarily. Away from the bank the water shallowed swift over a shelf of limestone and he went on upstream into the noise of the orewasher. The noise was dense, palpable, the fresh summer greenery seemed to almost vibrate with it. He went on into the churning wall of noise and nearer the washer the water grew turbulent, nigh opaque and in constant motion and roiled with sand and silt he could feel against his legs and in his shoes. He stopped, studying the water, a patient air of waiting about him.

The first fish was a sunperch bigger than a big man's hand and far bigger than his own. It came floating bellyup out of a clump of willows and he halffilled the bucket with water and, as if materializing near the surface, caught up the unsuspecting fish and bucketed it. Others then, an almost Biblical multitude of fishes. Whitesuckers and bass surfacing palely in miraculous fruition and he gathered them up steadily as a man picking cotton until the bucket was full.

The water near the washer and crusher did something to the fish, addled them, he would have said. He didn't know how, nor care. Times were hard in this year of 1947, as they had been in 1934, or for that matter in 1932, the year he had been born. He had learned early on that if food wanted to turn belly up and float into your waiting bucket you didn't analyze it. Times is hard, folks said, times is hard, a litany, a ritual, but few of these folk had known any other times save bad.

He waded back downstream with the thunder of the crusher diminishing perceptibly and through the cane and sawgrass to the chert roadbed, the water and fish sloshing heavily in the pail. He went on past the series of dead brick furnaces with their enormous flues rising smokeless and black against the hot brassy heavens like remnants of something lost. He passed the post office and the long clapboard company store and a sign that said Morgan Ironworks and past precarious shanties like jumbled lumber left by the recession of floodwaters and he saw no one about. Where a footpath wound toward Gander Ridge he left the footpath and took to the woods. Out of the hot weight of the sun and into deep shade. Beneath a walnut tree he halted and set down the pail. He wiped the sweat out of his eyes with his forearm and studied the fish with a professional eye. They were beginning to revive, moving sluggishly through the congested water, gills opening and closing, their sides slowly pulsating.

You've played hell now, ain't you? he asked the fish, dozed off in the creek and woke up somewhere you never been and don't know where in hell you got to and no road back.

He took up the fish and went on up the footpath past

a peeling yellow house with a packed earth yard impacted with flattened tin cans and bright blue glass shards and on into the smoky backyard where an old woman turned wildeyed from a steaming washpot of clothes she seemed to be stewing, screaming at him through the woodsmoke like a witch disturbed at her potions. She gestured threateningly with the stick she'd been worrying the clothes with.

You there, she screamed, ain't I told you about crossin my property.

He just waved dismissively onehanded and didn't turn.

You've been prowling through my stuff. What've you got in that bucket?

He still didn't turn. Mule turds, he said. You want one?

You nastymouthed little beast, she shrieked. I'll git you just as sure as you're born.

He'd heard all its variations before, and he went on. Gander Ridge sloped gradually upward through a sumac border where the blackberry briars had been arbitrarily leveled out to accommodate a series of faded section houses. The meager backyards abutted a bluff, the front sloped down to the road. Past the last house the railroad ran along a high rickrack embankment and beyond that in the distance the railroad trestle spanned the river.

He halted. He set the bucket of fish by his feet. Son of a bitch, he said. The last house was where he lived and there was a newlooking black Ford parked in the yard. He squatted for a moment and studied it. The sleek car before the shack looked temporary and anomolaic, poised for flight. It looked somehow predatory. It had been jacked up in the rear and it reminded him of a cat squatting on its haunches. He would have liked one just like it and he figured sometime he'd buy one.

All the same it presented a problem. He figured the car's driver for one of his mother's friends. His mother had a lot of friends, they came, they went. Friendships bloomed and withered with the exchange of coin of the realm, the sorrow of one's parting relieved by the joy of another's arrival.

Without really thinking about it much he had divided the friends into three main categories. There were the ones that totally ignored him. There were the ones who treated him with the vague and spurious kindness of a distant uncle you didn't see very much and perhaps couldn't quite recall your name. Sometimes they gave him a quarter and once one had given him a fatherly pat between his shoulders and told him he was growing into a regular little man. Then there were the mean ones. This comprised the larger category. They seem to think that with the transaction of the greasy dollar bills, he as well had been bought and paid for. They'd watch him with narrowed suspicious eyes. They'd develop an uncontrollable urge to slap him around some. Then they'd send him to widow Stovall's after whiskey and foollike he used to go. He generally poured out part of the whiskey, then pissed in it, a sordid and solitary vengeance, but a satisfactory one.

He had no way of knowing which kind this was and didn't want to know. He picked up the bucket and went on. He gave the house as wide a berth as the bluff permitted and turned up a hollow behind the house and followed a meandering stream.

The hollow rose in stony bluffs on either side and, where a spring flowed out of the rocks, he had constructed a homemade fishbox out of stone. He moved the sheet metal lid aside and poured the fish into the company of their more acclimated brothers. He chewed a sprig of peppermint and watched them. The icy waters of the spring seemed to rejuvenate them. They moved lazily through waving strands of the mossy bottom, goggleyed with perpetual wonder. He lifted his head to study the sun. It fell through the branches in a riot of greengold light and he judged it noonday, but he didn't figure there'd be any dinner.

By the middle of the afternoon he was wading Allen's Creek snake hunting with a slingshot. He had a round rock in the chamber and was scouting the lilypads, overhanging limbs and rocks where they'd likely be sunning for victims when he heard someone singing around a bend in the creek. He stepped back onto the bank and hunkered in the encroaching brush, peering through willow fronds. Broken light fell in a shimmering silver sheet on the bend in Allen's Creek and a girl walked into it. He knew every girl on Allen's Creek, yet he had never seen her before. She was humming softly to herself. She had pale fine hair and the sun gave it a curious halo effect. She was carrying in one hand a bouquet of Tiger Lilies and with the other holding her dress aloft out of the water. He sat for a moment studying her intently and thinking no thoughts at all. He seemed to be photographing her with his mind, the darkly tanned calves of her legs, the long expanse of her white thighs somehow shocking. There was something magically angelic about the way the sun haloed her hair, and something dark and unnamable twisted in him like a knife. Without articulating it, he felt she was too perfect for the imperfect world he moved through and without thinking he raised the slingshot and took quick aim and fired. The rock struck her hard on the left thigh and she lurched and cried out and dropped the flowers. She had almost fallen. Oh shit, he said. He was already sorry and he couldn't figure why he'd done it.

He plunged across the shoal in a rising fan of water toward her, gathering up the Tiger Lilies as he went. He pressed them into her hand but she flung them away, stood rubbing her leg. There was an eggsized welt on her inner thigh. She was crying, her eyes were blue and pained, her face white and flattened by the weight of the sun. He could see the delicate beads of moisture on her upper lip. Shit, I'm sorry, he told her. Let me see. She raised her dress further and he gently moved her hands away and massaged the reddened bruise. At the touch of his hand she involuntarily clasped her legs together and for a moment they stood so, his hand imprisoned between her thighs. She swayed in the swift kneedeep water, suddenly grasped his shoulders with a hand to each to steady herself. I swear I didn't mean to, he told her earnestly. His voice sounded strange to him. There was a faroff but insistent ringing in his ears. He could feel the hot weight of her thighs, on either side of his hand and his thumb rested against the crotch of her underwear. He rubbed her leg gently. I was just shootin at a snake, he told her.

Well don't you make a pretty picture, a voice said. I wish I had a camera. Wouldn't Grandma like to see this.

He started jerking his hand free of her clasped thighs as if they'd seared it. Lillie Mae Stovall was standing on the creekbank watching them, little shoebutton eyes bright with selfsatisfied malice. Wait'll I tell what you done.

I wasn't doin nothing, Yates said.

No? Well, you was just before it. What you wasn't doin yet was on your mind and the Bible says thinkin it and doin it's the same thing.

He wondered could he whip her. She was big, stolid to the third power. Somehow loathsome in her shapeless dress, hair wound in intricate pigtails, her entire body incandescent with malevolent glee, hands clinched in outsize fists, Got you now, she said. I been waitin for somethin on you and now I got it. Cassie just came up from Alabama to live with us and you done tried to rape her, and her a orphan. Grandma is goin to purty beat the shit out of you. Then she's goin to tell your mama and you'll get it beat out of you again. You'll be sorry you ever heard of a baby rabbit.

His heart went heavy as a stone. He had forgotten the rabbits, and on top of that, this girl was living with Grandma Stovall, and he instantly discarded all the possibilities he'd been entertaining. It was on his tongue to beg her not to tell but he choked his unspoken pleas. It tasted bitter and dry as ashes. It was a waste of time and he wouldn't give her the satisfaction. Then tell her, he said.

I aim to.

The girl, Cassie, had waded out of the creek. She stood beside Lillie, wringing water out of the back of her skirt. He really wasn't doing anything, Lillie, she said.

It may not be nothin in Alabama, but up here in Tennessee it looked like he was rubbin between your legs, Lillie said. Or my eyes may be failin me. Either way we'll tell Granny and let her sort it out.

I forgot, Yates said. I got some money.

This evinced some interest. How much? Lillie asked.

He was fetching up from inside his trousers his homemade moneybelt, a Country Gentleman tobacco sack tied with seagrass string. They counted it on a sandbar. Twenty-seven pennies, aligned in five stacks of five each and two odd. It'd buy several pieces of candy, he said encouragingly.

She seemed to weigh this. For a while it seemed she was going to take the bribe and then she regretfully shook her head. She pushed the pennies toward him with a rawboned hand. It just ain't enough, she said. I'd like to, but it ain't enough.

Why goddamn you, Yates said. He was gathering up pennies and sand and stuffed his wallet. Goddamn you and that old bat both, and you can tell her I said so.

Lillie Mae had arisen, stood placidly dusting the sand off her dress.

I will, she said.

As the crow flies it is not far from Alabama to Allen's Creek, Tennessee, but the distance from Town Creek, Alabama, to the attic room of the Muledick Saloon is unreckonable.

Nights she'd lie in her cot and wonder how she could have come to such a pass. She remembered the cool clean smell of freshly cut grass, the sound of an early morning boat on the river, the look of skies that seemed to know no shade save clear blue. Remembered her father in his crisp blue uniform, her mother in a white linen dress. The year she was fifteen her father and mother had been returning from a New Year's Eve party up on a backwoods whiskey still when a drunk had been seized by some dark impulse and veered across the centerline and slammed them head on. They were dead before the highway patrol arrived and her life had been destroyed as surely as if her flesh and bone had been caught between the rending metal.

She'd heard folks say you can't take it with you, but her father had always considered himself a resourceful man and had managed to do that. He had taken the smooth green lawn, the sweet slow Sunday picnics, the quiet afternoon drives, her mother. He had taken it all into the casket his brothers had consigned to the church. He had taken the way she had known, who she was, a girl who was going to finish high school in Town Creek and go away to Mobile or Birmingham for a few years of college and return to Town Creek and teach elementary school and marry some day when she found the right man. All that had been taken and stuffed and pounded into the box and the lid forced shut. She wasn't that person anymore.

The person she was went to live with relatives where she was welcome but not quite wanted. She began to unravel around the edges, to ease tentatively onto the wild side. She took to slipping out at night with the boys to joyride. The long straight highway coming at you at ninety through a blur of bootleg whiskey. Her naked breasts in the moonlight, hot clumsy kisses at her throat. After awhile they couldn't hold her anymore and they sent her on somewhere else. Ultimately, she'd been sent to her grandmother's, the black sheep of all their family, a sheep so utterly black as to be invisible on a moonless night.

She don't want you, Lillie Mae said out of the dark.

She didn't answer. Sometimes if she didn't answer Lillie Mae would reckon her asleep and finally she would shut up.

Nobody wants you, Lillie Mae said.

She lay still in her bed and tried to sleep. Far off there was a train whistle. An owl cried.

She only took you in on account of the money, Lillie Mae said. They send her money every month just to keep you here. You must be worthless as shit for folks to pay good money just to have you live somewhere else.

Lillie Mae was sly and devious and sometimes she kept prodding and prodding like a doctor. Does this hurt, can you feel this? What happens when I press here?

Me and granny don't want you neither, she said.

Who cares? she said, and she could have bitten her tongue off. Who would want you too? I'd worry about myself if you did. There'd have to be something awful about me to make you all want me.

I'll bet that boy was all over your titties, too, and you was lettin him feel wherever he wanted to.

Well. You just wish he was feelin yours.

You goddamned little whore you.

Goddamned whore yourself.

Lillie Mae chuckled deep in her throat. You're not such a Miss Priss as you'd like to be, she said.

She just lay quite still and pretended to sleep. The train whistle looped on, distant till it honed away to nothing and gave way to a steady cry of insect sounds, the raucous laughter of a drunk. I am from Town Creek, she thought. I am in the Muledick Saloon, she thought in wonder. I am living in the attic of a place I would not even pronounce the name of aloud. Maybe I am in the waiting room of hell just listening for someone to open the door and call out my name.

She watched from the high attic window the comings and goings at what had become her home. Drunkards and lechers and gamblers and malcontents of every stripe, begrimed and sweating and reeking of mules and bootleg whiskey and just the very tawdriness of their lives. Sometimes the men gave Granny money and Lillie would arise and accompany them into the night. Looking at Cassie with a curious flounce of pride, the look of a wallflower girl at the prom being asked to dance by the captain of the football team.

At first, she'd seen them trooping in and out of the parlor, such a steady stream of tainted commerce that she guessed the old woman was the only one on Allen's Creek making a lot of money. Not that anyone ever saw any of it. The old woman didn't trust banks and she didn't trust people. The only person she trusted was herself and she was squirreling the money away somewhere.

She began to fear Granny. This squat, reptilian evil little dwarf of a woman. You can be appalled only so long at a time, she thought, and the thought carried a seed of fear. Familiarity breeds not contempt but acceptance.

Don't make me, she thought. Don't ever make me or somehow I'll manage to kill you in your sleep, I swear it.

The tromping of heavy feet, the scuffle of falling struggling bodies, raucous laughter. She'd sit by the window hourslong and listen to the call of the whippoorwills and there seemed something clean about them, timeless. They'd called before man struggled up out of the slime, they'd call when ultimately, he waded back into it. It didn't matter to them, they were above it all. They talked ceaselessly as if measuring the night with their cries.

She read and reread her books. They seemed of little use to her, they bore no relevance to her life. In simpler times, she'd seen herself as the heroine of these stories and she judged that now with contempt. Lillie, Maid of Astolat, was working out of the top floor of the Muledick Saloon. Arthur was off on the crusades, he didn't write and didn't write. Snow White had fallen among thieves and the Seven Dwarfs were drunken lechers and smellsmocks and their devices were out of a gothic horror novel.

She'd lie on the bed and try to go to sleep before Lillie Mae came up. Fearful always of footsteps on the stairs.

She thought of being a little girl that seemed someone else in another life at Sunday school, but she remembered the smell of furniture polish on the pews, the dusty sanctified smell of the worn hymnals, Aqua Velva on her father's freshly shaven cheek when he leaned to kiss her. Pious voices raised in song. Are you washed in the blood of the lamb?

She lay composed, eyes closed, arms clasped loosely across her stomach. Composed not for death but for life, to be born, for something to happen. She thought of Yates. His naïve face a blank paper on which to make your mark. He thought he knew everything but in truth every day was a whole new world. There was something endearing about this thought and she fell asleep.

He was in Dow Cook's eating a package of peanuts and drinking a Coca-Cola. His jaws stopped chewing the peanuts when she came in. She crossed the room swiftly to the counter and handed Dow a list. He began to gather her purchases and align them on the counter. Yates watched. Cataloguing these items, half a dozen eggs, sugar, a bottle of vanilla extract. She kept her eyes toward Dow and the front of the store. There was something decorous and studiedly unobtrusive in her manner, as if she were practicing to become invisible. Yates didn't miss a move she made.

When Dow had her groceries bagged she handed him a bill and tied the change he gave her in a handkerchief, put it carefully in her pocket, and took up the bag.

Yates hadn't thought she noticed he was even in the

world, but she didn't miss much. As she crossed the room
she glanced at him, nodded formally and gave him an enig-
matic half smile that so disrupted his perception of time
that she was already out the door and the screen slapped to
before he came to himself. When he did he was up immediately. Opportunity or what passed for it in these provinces
had knocked but tentatively once and he didn't expect it to
happen again.

She was just going down the steps.

Hey there, he said.

She lifted a hand goodbye and went on down the
steps. She was already quickening her steps to cross the
road when he called again.

Hey.

She stopped.

Let me carry that sack for you.

That's all right. It's real light. Thanks anyway though.
It's sweet of you to offer.

Sweet, he thought. Aloud he said: You ain't making a
cake are you?

Me? No, it's just some stuff I picked up for Granny.

She'll turn that sugar to salt and rot them eggs just by
touchin em. You better keep her away from that flavorin
too.

I got to get on.

Say I may be comin up there to see you.

Do what?

I may come up there to call on you. You think that'd
be all right?

Lord no. I think it'd be everything in the world but all
right. Granny's made all kinds of threats what she's goin
to do.

Leave Granny's threats out of it. I ain't afraid of no little turtlefaced woman, Yates said. I faced down grown men

over less than this. What do you think about me comin?

About what?

About me comin.

Well you do whatever you think you got to do. But I got to get on.

Just don't be surprised if you see me.

She didn't answer. She went on.

Hey, I ain't had me no cake in a long time, he yelled after her.

He knocked and waited awhile. Maybe she ain't even here, Yates thought. Maybe the old bat's died and they've all gone to the buryin. Maybe there's not even anybody here but Cassie. He heard footsteps. The door jerked inward and the old woman herself stood there glaring at him in disbelief. She appeared to be struck dumb by his very appearance. He just glared back: there was something turtlelike about her. Her nose and chin suggested a hooked snout, her bright little reptilian eyes seemed never to blink. There was a sour reek of swampwater about her.

God almighty, she said. She opened her mouth to say more, then snapped it to and kept on staring at him.

In truth he was something to see. He'd slicked his hair back until the curls were plastered to his gleaming skull and he'd blacked his shoes with shoe polish purloined from Dow Cook's and for some reason he appeared to have shaved. There was the sickly reek of attar of roses about him.

God almighty. Is that lard on your head?

Hell no it ain't lard. It's cloverine salve, if it's anything to you. Is Cassie here?

What?

Is Cassie here? I come to see her.

Damned if you ain't about the sweetest smelling thing I've ever come across. I've got a good mind to just keep you. Stand you in a corner somewhere just to freshen up the place.

Behind her the room lay in a serried gloom: Two men he didn't know sat on a shadowed couch. There was a five-gallon glass jug of some darklooking liquid sitting before them and one of the men removed the lid and dipped a cup into it with something akin to ceremony and drank. Above the cup he watched Yates with a bemused curiosity. Yates didn't see Cassie.

Just what did you have in mind, if you don't mind my askin.

I just came to see Cassie. Just whatever, to sit awhile I reckon.

They'll be wearin overcoats in hell before you set your gimlet ass in my front room. If you ain't got the beatenest nerve of anybody I ever come across. If you hadn't took me by surprise, I'd done wore a broom out over you. You git off of my property or I'll have one of these highfinders here put you off of it.

I ain't one to butt in where I ain't wanted, Yates said. But I don't back down as easy as I used to and any highfinder lays a hand on me is lookin to lose it.

She slammed the door.

He stood there a time as if he didn't quite know what his next move should be then he went back down the steps.

I ain't got no advice to the lovelorn, Crowe said. I don't know what to tell you.

I thought a man of your varied background might be able to figure somethin out. You bein a ex-schoolteacher and all.

In all my varied background I don't believe I ever come across anything quite like you, Crowe said, standing to one side grinning sardonically. It's a waste of your time anyhow. If she looks half as good as you say she does some highroller'll sign her up for the moving pictures. She'll be out in Hollywood screwing big shots and you'll still be here stealin chickens and fightin with her grandma. It all just sounds like a waste of time to me.

But what would you do?

Does she have a mind of her own or does she do everything her grandma says?

She's got a mind I reckon like everybody else but Granny never lets her out of her sight. It's just because it's me. Me and Granny never have been what you'd call real close.

He'd been helping Crowe saw heaterwood with a crosscut saw and now they were loading it into Crowe's wagon.

What you've got to do then is get in good with the old woman. Make her like you. But the main thing is when a man goes courtin he's got to have prospects.

Prospects?

Yeah. Like money, a good job, a good education. Figure out a way to make somethin of yourself so it'll show you can take care of her good.

I ever got a chance I'd take care of her good. Better

than any other of these hardankles around here.

Yeah. But you got to admit you're a little shy in the prospects department. In fact I'd say the prospects of an apprentice troglodyte like yourself are dismal to the point of nonexistent.

What's a troglodyte?

A cave dweller like yourself.

I been thinkin some about what you said about gettin in good with her. Just in a general way. I was thinkin what if I could come up with some way to save her life. You know, figger some way to get her in a spot where it looks for sure like she's goin to die. Then at the last minute I'd step in and save her life. She'd be all over me then. But knowin me if I ever seen her in such a spot I'd just back off and I'd chicken out at the last minute, throw up my hands, and just let the bitch die.

Just before nightfall clouds rose in the west and a thunderhead boiled upward out of it and lay like a malignant tumor above the darkening horizon. Lights flared and died about its base and flared again, but Yates could hear no thunder yet. He sat on the ridge overlooking the house and waited for the rain which would suit his purpose very well. He had a rolled burlap bag pillowed beneath his head. He lay on an outcropping of stone beneath a dead beech and through its dead branches he idly studied the sky. Stars one by one came palely out of the dark, burned through the fabric of night, brightened more yet, a pale band of them like jewelry strewn in petulant anger. Then the seeping stain of dark clouds in the keep of high fast winds inundated them and they were gone. Perversely, brief night ended not by daybreak but by still deeper darkness.

He had no way of knowing the time but he judged it midnight, or near it, when he moved. He arose and with a rock cradled under his arm sauntered down around the bluff on some old nearlost footpath that led to the house. The first drops of rain were singing in the trees and he'd begun to hear the first thunder, faint and faroff, a distant hollow rumbling rolling baleful, muttering down the stone corridors of the bluffs framing the river. The woods thinned and ended abruptly, and he could see the dark bulk of the house, lightning at its darkened windows with illusory brightness.

When he stepped into the yard a dog erupted from the porch in a flurry of fierce barking. Yates faded back into the brush and squatted there with his crokersack and the softball sized chunk of stone he'd picked up. Come on, he thought. Come on out here, Sport, and I'll rub that head for you. I'll lay you out like a hog with its throat cut.

The dog went on and on but it didn't leave the edge of the porch. After a time Yates heard someone yell shut up but it didn't. Then the door opened slightly inward, a rectangle of darkness deeper still. On it, a pale wraith-like shape printed itself like a moving image forming on a photographic plate. A man in long underwear strode onto the porch and came to its edge and stood peering into the night. Short stocky old man with grizzled yellowgray whiskers. Yates couldn't see his face good, like a spectre in the rain stringing off the roof.

Yet he knew the face. It was the face out of a child-hood nightmare, Death's head peering into a nighttime window, the grim reaper prowling the yard. He'd seen it once in his yard on a December night long ago and he'd seen it at Dow Cook's store and he'd seen it in his dreams.

He wondered suddenly if his father had crouched here awaiting deeper dark to steal the side of meat, if he too had studied Stagg's face, and he felt unreal. Time seemed to be repeating itself, to be twisting on its coils like a serpent. He was caught in some ritualistic reenactment of history he couldn't control.

Then a sense of power touched him. He thought, I could have changed it. I could have killed you. I could have slipped in and killed you where you slept for shotgunning my Pa. I ort to. But I reckon I'll let you live. I can't right everybody's wrongs, all this stuff happened a long time ago and I can't fix it. I got only so much time and I got my own wrongs to straighten out.

The man said, You, shut your goddamn mouth. The dog fell into an uneasy silence, studying the woods where Yates squatted. The man fumbled with his clothing and urinated into the muddy earth yard then turned and went back inside and pushed the door to.

When Yates eased out of the border of blackjack oaks the dog commenced again in short happy barks. The man seemed to have been waiting crouched behind the door. It fairly sprang inward, and the man ran onto the porch and kicked the dog in the slats. It yelped in outrage and leapt off the porch into the rain and slunk under the shelter of the porch. The man gave the woods a cursory look and went back in and slammed the door, and this time the dog didn't bark even when Yates came out tossing the stone like a pitcher warming up, crossed around the house to another smaller building. He went through a slab and chickenwire gate into fetid and ammonia smelling darkness.

He laid the rock and crokersack down and dried his hands as best he could on the sack. He took from a pocket a glass bottle and uncorked it and tipped out a match and struck it on the tin roof. It flared and guttered and died. Another showed him long poles nailed on slab braces, a row of chickens browsing shoulder to shoulder. He looked about to fix things in his mind and dropped the match when it burned his fingers. Photoelectric light flickered strobic through the slatted walls and he took up the rock and moved toward the roosting chickens.

They quarreled sleepily as he felt among them, selecting by feel. Dreaming their chicken dreams to the mesmeric drumming of the rain on the tin and so rudely disrupted. There now, he whispered, no pushin and shoving. Everbody can't go. I've only got so big a sack and I don't want yins to smother.

When the sack was burdened to what he considered a satisfactory yet safe level he went out with it into the rain, then went back and got the rock in case the dog's interest in him had been awakened. It hadn't. He crossed the yard beneath the dark bowl of stormy night to the edge of the sheltering woods, then without knowing he was going to, whirled back toward the house and threw the stone as hard as he could. It struck a window taking glass and weatherrotted sash and all and the commotion seemed enormous. He watched, crouched in the scrub listening for cries of outrage, gunfire, anything but all that came out of the appalled silence was the soft drumming of the rain.

Within the hour he was far downriver sheltered beneath an enormous outcropping of bluff and he had attained a great measure of comfort. The fire he'd built of weatherdried stumps had died to a pulsing bed of orange coals and over these coals a chicken roasted on a spit of green hickory. Yates basted the chicken with its own fat and drops of hot fat slid off the chicken into the coals and burned with brief blue spurts of flame. The smell of the chicken roasting was almost unbearable. His clothes

steamed where he'd draped them to dry and behind him
the chickens muttered furiously to themselves in their
crokersack home, spaced carefully to prevent them from
smothering. Money in the bank.

He ate the chicken leant against a boulder staring off
downriver where the storm tracked northward, the storm-
cloud domeshaped and metallooking when the lightning
arced out of it. Faroff he could see the river uncoiling and
the trees on the bluff writhing in the wind. He was warm
and dry and feeling for once fulfilled and comfortable.
He sat looking out over the expanse of tumultuous world
the lightning showed him. He was pleased with himself, a
small and ill-kept country squire watching off his makeshift stone balcony all his works and finding them not un-
pleasing.

He seemed the only soul there was in all the world,
the first to be or the last remaining. Through the blowing
curtain of rain, the flaring lightning remarked only stone
and trees, fire on water. The world looked primitive and
atavistic and there was nothing in all that he could see of
the works of man.

It rained all night. The pale dawn came almost unnoticed and it rained fitfully still. Through the mist and rainy
fog of daybreak he threaded his way down the bluff and
out into a fallow bottom on which a makeshift logroad
meandered and finally ended at the train. He crossed the
trestle pausing once and setting down the sack and leaning to study the river. The water was swift and yellow-
looking, tree branches and leaves and castoff car tires
rolled blackly in the current, once an entire tree appeared
uprooted and bound downriver. He watched it until the
river's swift clocking made him dizzy, then he took up the
sack and went on.

He met the peddler upriver, waiting in a concrete

culvert higher than he was tall. When he heard the sound of the truck he clambered out and halted the peddler with an upraised arm.

High rattletrap truck of faded orange, a makeshift chickenwire cage cobbled onto the back where fretted a gaggle of chickens and one lone duck. The sardonic wizened old man greeted Yates with a jaundiced eye.

Yates climbed the steps to the interior of the truck, a pickup truck so crude it seemed to have been hewed from a single block of metal with a chopping axe, homemade shelves lined with merchandise of every stripe. Yates's eyes darting about these shelved goods, cataloging all these wonders. Who knows what miracles, hammered silver from Spain perhaps, silk and jade from the Orient.

It was a hell of a storm last night, he told the peddler without preamble. Lightnin strikin trees. Most wind I ever seed. The river's up, too.

I reckon I slept through it, the peddler said without much interest. Workin people got to be abed at night. Can't run the woods all night, sleep all day like a loafer like you. Let's buy or sell one. Which are you doin? You buyin?

Sellin, Yates said, handing him the sack.

The peddler took the sack, peered into the depths. Yates was studying the jarred candy, the crated popbottles. Breathing in the strange spicy odor of the peddler's wares.

Whose are they?

They're mine. Or will be till I sell em to you.

I mean whose was they then?

They was always mine, Yates said.

The peddler was weighing the chickens, nestling them one at a time on his grocer's scale. Yeah, he said I reckon that's why you met me a mile or two out of your way. So nobody'd see you sellin your chickens.

Yates was unperturbed. Truth is they're wild chickens, he said. I just caught em up here. They in a herd like
wildhorses does and this is just where the herd was.

You ever figger chickens is just goin to take over?
the peddler said. Without you to keep em thinned out they
just goin have the run of Allen's Creek.

He tolled up figures. I make three dollars and twelve
cents, the peddler said. Yates's eyes watched him fetch
up money from his apron pockets. You want it in cash or
merchandise?

He selected two candy bars and a popcola and took
the rest in change, comforting weight of the pocket
against his leg. The peddler hesitated, fetched up another
quarter and a fifty-cent piece. You want to make seventy-five cents?

Is the feller I have to kill big or little? Yates asked. If
he's little I might think on it.

From a box the peddler took a stack of thin yellow
handbills. I took on the job of handin these out but I'm
runnin behind this morning. I figured I'd just sub it out
to you.

How much did you take it on for? Yates asked cagily.

It ain't nothing to you what I took it on for. I'm offering you seventy-five cents.

I'll take it, Yates said, reaching for the money and
sheaf of handbills.

He went back down the steps reading the topmost
handbill. It seemed to tell of a circus in Ackerman's Field.
The peddler followed him down the steps and was caging
the chickens at the rear of the truck.

It's enough of them handbills for every man, woman
and child on Allen's Creek, the peddler said. Every soul
gets one. Don't leave nobody out. Don't throw none away.

All right, Yates said.

Put one up in Dow Cook's window and one in the post office and carry some up to the Muledick to give out to them drunks up there. You'll have plenty.

All right, Yates said again. He was walking along still studying the handbill.

Boy, I got a market for black root, the peddler called after him. You aim to dig me some this year?

I reckon so, Yates said.

Mayapple too? I need a lot of mayapple.

I may dig some black root but I ain't foolin with no mayapple. Dig a towsack full and you done nothin but waste your time. I'll scratch shit with the chickens before I'll dig mayapple.

Well, yeah, the peddler said, closing the cage. Big livestock dealer like you.

Crouched in the culvert he unwrapped a candy bar. He chewed slowly, making it last, and read the topmost handbill. *Tangelli's Traveling Circus*, the headline read. Against a circus backdrop a black panther seemed to be leaping off the handbill into Yates's lap. It seemed to him a marvelous rendering. It appeared in motion. Its ears were flattened against its skull, its eyes yellow slits, paws outstretched with claws unsheathed to strike. In the background a multitude of tents were silhouetted, and a black Ferris wheel tilted against a yellow sky. Below the cat, script told of wonders on the midway, freakshows, dancing girls, death defying acts on the highwire.

Goddamn what a cat, he breathed. He had stopped

chewing to study the cat and now he opened the dope and took a swallow. I aim to see that cat, he said absently as he looked at the handbill next then thumbed through them but they all seemed identical.

He came out and went on back toward Allen's Creek, the weight of the money a small warmth in his pocket. He stopped again on the trestle and watched the roiling river. It seemed to have risen, seeped yellowly out into the bottomland. He folded the top handbill and put it into his shirt pocket. One by one he began to drop the others toward the river, watching the wind take them like drifting leaves. Then he dropped the rest of the stack, a cloud of them billowing out in the wind, a strange rain of black panthers fluttering into the swift muddy water and gone.

He came into Allen's Creek to the hammering of the washer rocking, the smell of woodsmoke. The smoke from dying morning cookfires hovering the ground in the damp heavy air. The smell of burning cedar. There was something fiercely evocative about it, some lost memory of his childhood that tried to overtake and reclaim him and did not want to let him be.

He shook it off. He thought of the handbill and glanced at the row of faded yellow sectionhouses scattered about the muddy thoroughfare.

It's a circus, he thought, and not a one of you son of a bitches knows it but me.

Cassie slipped away from Granny Stovall and met him. They walked down the creek and lay on a white sandbar and idly watched the flooded creek hurrying to the river.

She studied the handbill and gave it back to him. It seemed to mean less to her than it did to him, and he could not have explained the cat's importance. There was a vast enormity looming below his consciousness but he could not articulate it.

I aim to take you to that circus, he said. We aim to see that cat. I got some money.

She watched him languidly, her eyes sleepylooking in the hot sun and not uncatlike themselves. Her eyes were bluegreen and longlashed and he could never fathom what she was thinking. When she smiled, he could see the clean white line of her teeth. There was something wise and timeless in her smile. She seemed to have been born knowing things he didn't even suspect yet.

How you plannin on gettin me there?

I ain't quite figured that part out yet.

Reckon you could tote me on your back?

I'll figure somethin out.

I seen a circus in Huntsville once, a great big one. They had everthing. Little place like Ackerman's Field, likely this is just a little bitty circus anyway.

Little bitty ones don't have them cats like that, he said.

She fell silent, seemed to be thinking about something. After a time she said, This circus had a person that was half man and half woman.

I never heard of such. Was it man on the top and woman on the bottom or what?

She smiled. It wasn't like that. They said it had a, she paused, a little thing like a boy's got and like a woman too. I guess. I don't know. They wouldn't let me see it, I wadn't old enough. You had to be grown to get in.

Yates couldn't picture such a being. To be so marvelously overendowed that folks would pay to see you. He pondered the logistics of its reproduction.

They called it a morphodite or somethin, she said.

He'd have asked more but somehow this conversation embarrassed him. It seemed not fitting. There were things he'd like to have asked that he suspected she'd know but a curious part of him did not want her to. Anyway, the panther was what interested him. It seemed foreign and mysterious, an avatar of all that existed beyond the rock bluffs ringing Allen's Creek.

She arose. I got to be getting back. You want to walk me back part way?

He got up, reluctantly. Lately he had fallen to planning some revenge he might take against Granny Stovall. She troubled his dreams. I hate that old ratfaced bat, he said.

She took his hand. Some mild electric current seemed to rejuvenate him. He could actually feel his spirits lifting.

Can't you slip out tonight? It'll be warm. We could go up by the washer and swim naked.

I don't know, she said. I'll ask Granny. I'll get away from her one of these days.

We got to go to that circus. We might even go see a picture show. They got one.

She just shook her head, smiled wistfully. When I go it'll be a lot further than a picture show, she said. I'm goin to Chicago. I'm goin where there's money and fine clothes and everbody has a car to drive.

Would you go if I could take you to Chicago?

She laughed. She swung on his arm. I'd go to Chicago with a morphodite, she said. If one asked me I'd ask when and be packed and ready.

Somehow this wasn't what Yates expected. If I see one headed north I'll tell him about you, he said sourly.

Perched on the edge of a canebottom chair, he drank coffee while Black Crowe fried a pan of potatoes. Past the windows of Crowe's cabin, dark blue dusk was falling and bullbats bisected the purple shadows of the garden.

You want some of this?

Yates found a tin plate. I reckon, he said. I had chicken last night though.

I ain't got no chicken, Crowe said. It's this or nothin.

Between the two I'll take taters ever time, Yates said, filling his plate. What I ought to've done was to lie me one or two of em out. Foollike I sold em all. I need the money though. What I may do is get me a start of em and raise my own.

What you may do is get your skinny ass blown clean off with a shotgun. That's far more likely in my judgment. What's your plan, to start with chicken rustling and kindly work your way up the ladder of crime toward murderin and rapin and such?

I don't have a plan yet, Yates said. I just play em like they fall. You see one of these? They gettin a circus in Ackerman's Field. He laid down his fork and unpocketed the handbill. He unfolded and laid it on the table before Crowe.

Crowe studied it a moment. This is the only one I've seen. Usually they got em up everwhere.

There ain't no more, Yates said.

It must be a damn small circus to only run off one handbill, Crowe said. But you seem to have circus on the brain, so I guess they got it into the right hands.

You want to go with me?

My circus days is long gone. But don't let that stop

you. Ever boy ought to see a circus one time anyway.

I been thinkin about joinin up. Boy that'd be the life. Travelin here and yonder. Eatin hot dogs ever night. Watchin them hootchie cootchie dancers. Do them circuses stay on the go all the time?

I think they winter down in Florida somewhere, Crowe said. Boy, what'd you ever do in a circus? That ain't no life.

I might be a clown, Yates said. He grinned. Do me a death defyin act on the highwire.

Boy, you don't need no highwire, he said. Your very life is an act of death defiance. You're the most accident-prone person I ever seen. You don't plan nothin. You don't look ahead. You just take it as it comes. Even when it falls into your lap, you just piss it away.

Yates got up to go. He was refolding his handbill. Well I reckon I could learn from you, he said. Then I could get a bluff blowed up from under me and hang upside down in a pine tree from my leg. I reckon that be fun.

Don't get huffy, Crowe grinned. You got to see wrong before you'll know right.

BOOK II

ACKERMAN'S FIELD

The train went on into the falling night past farmers and past rich fields heavy with corn, past weary sharecroppers who'd let night fall on them leading their mules from the darkening fields, past leaning clapboard shanties yellowlit against whatever prowled out there in the darkness. There in the barren rooms the weary sharecroppers sought for the night to replace what the day had stolen and, in the hot charged darkness, they dreamed their tangled dreams. He went on past weatherbeaten country stores with their rusted gaspumps, attendant and highballing on into the flatlands.

Faroff against the blurred foothills he could see the feeble lights of houses and he hadn't known there was so much of the world, so much of life that was out of reach, that he couldn't know. Each light a house, a family, gathered about the hearth and aligned against the dark, each house a thousand stories he'd never hear. All these lives would play out their string without him, never even know he was rolling through the night. He felt an aching longing for the timbre of their voices, the communion of their eyes, the acknowledgment that he belonged. Then the sights vanished, elongated with speed like stars streaking down the night, as lost and irrevocable as Saint Elmo's Fire roiled in seawater. Then he was curving downward, the cars swaying, blueblack boles of trees flicking fast like pickets in a fence, leaves drifting in a whirlwind from the violence of their passage and a kind of nervous elation seized him. He was streaking down into the world of men whether it wanted him or not.

After awhile a fecund yellow moon cradled up above the cypress and paced him, riding above him so close he felt he could touch its remote face. After awhile the train began to slow and, peering through the slatted walls, he could see houses coming more frequent, and beyond a long fanshaped chain of trees a cluster of them grouped together in a hamlet. He was up and about immediately and, when the train had almost come to the depot, he was off and running, falling once and cursing and running back up the tracks. The train halted with a metallic shriek and, with an eye out for anyone in a position of authority in the night, he sauntered along the gravel toward town on a path that wound through the weedgrown tieyard adjacent to the railroad tracks. He saw no one about and began to wonder where everybody was. Perhaps they'd fled in some vast exodus pouring westward like lemmings.

He didn't tarry long. Such stores as he found were shuttered and barred. He trod the board sidewalk for a time, peering in their windows, but whatever marvels they held were glassed out of his reach and at length he turned back toward the tieyard, drawn to the known out of all this vast unknown when somewhere overhead an explosion racked the firmament and he leapt and swore and his foreshortened shadow seemed charred, burning, writhing onto the wooden sidewalk beneath his feet. He peered up, eyes wide and wonderstruck into the blackness where green and red fire toiled away in showers of burning phosphorous until the sparks died and the skies were blacker than he'd ever seen them. Another burst illuminating a vast drifting octopus of smoke like the dark spectral shade of the one previous and the sky was lit by a vast medusa of fire, colored serpents writhing in the darkness with gold and silver cascading downward as a pyramid of fire covered the horizon.

He'd seen the arcing trajectory of this one and figured to track it to its source. He turned and followed the sidewalk past darkened houses wavering in uncertain light to what appeared to be a fenced-in field. The pulsing sky showered sparks down on a series of tents and a Ferris wheel turning gaudily like a waterwheel in a river and a shapeless crowd of people aligned against a board fence and an expanse of mowed field in the center of which men crouched like alchemists of old battling over their position, then sparks spewed and the men backed quickly away and all eyes followed the artillery shell skyward where the night went white in a flickering photoelectric light and there was a nighdeafening concussive explosion.

He found a gap in the fence where an old whitehaired man sat in attendance in a folding chair. The old bored-looking man was sucking on a stump of a cigar and fondling the cigar box of tickets he held in his lap.

I come to see the cat, Yates said.

The midway and the sideshows is done closed, the ticket-taker said. Be open again tomorrow. We havin the fireworks display tonight though.

I reckon I'll just watch that then, Yates said.

The man was proffering a yellow ticket. It's a quarter, he said.

Yates had the quarter half out then abruptly repocketed it. I doubt I could see any better on that side of the fence than I can from this side, he said.

Hey, you can't do that less you pay the quarter, the man said.

How come?

Cause it costs a quarter to see it, the man explained patiently.

Why shitfire, Yates said, they can't stop me from lookin up. How bout if I just look at the sky and promise to shut my eyes every time one goes off?

I hate a damned smartass kid like you, the man said. There are too many of you, this world would be a sight better off if your daddy had been cut before he ever come across your mother.

Yates just turned away toward the field and leant against a fencepost watching the sky in its cataclysmic turmoil and after awhile the old man unpocketed an enormous watch and studied it and arose. He folded the chair, tucked it under one arm and ambled away toward the tents with the cigar box of tickets.

After awhile the sky grew dark and still and remained silent. Yates waited but the men had arisen and were deserting through the field. The crowd stirred reluctantly. The sky stayed dark and unbroken. The crowd had separated and was moving slowly toward the gap in the fence and he guessed the show over and was glad he hadn't wasted a quarter on so meager a portion of it. Folks were passing him through the gap and he joined them, a crowd that seemed of an enormous and weighty silence, struck mute by the lateness of the hour or perhaps the visions they'd been permitted, countrylooking in overalls and gingham, towing children in whose eyes the ashes of wonder still burned.

He followed the crowd back to town uncertain of his bearings until he knew where he was, then he angled again toward the tieyard. He figured no one would bother him here and was proven right. He lay atop a tie pile feeling the cool wood pressing his shirt against his back.

Tabled so beneath the quiet heavens, he lay with his arms crossed like an offering to the pinpricks of unfamiliar heavens. Even the firmament seemed different here in the cities of men. The constellations, turning like great bejeweled carnival rides were strangers to him, more wonders than he had ever seen. It was a long time before he fell asleep.

He was up and about with first light and there were other folk stirring as well and he guessed that Saturday was a big deal for commerce in Ackerman's Field. He went up beyond the sticks of crossties curing in the sun and across the railroad tracks into an alley running behind tall brick buildings. He went past enormous stacks of brown beerbottles and when he came out of the alley, a yellow dog padded along behind him, its red tongue lolling. The dog followed him in a tentative way as if prepared to whirl and run should he reach for a rock.

He went in the first store he came to, cruising the aisles, as if to see what merchandise these outland stores carried. An old man watched with a suspicious eye and he went out without buying anything. He figured he wasn't so hard up he'd buy from a man who watched you like a sneakthief.

He went on up the street. Sidewalks here of oak planking nailed to sills. At a vacant lot before the hotel three buggies were parked and three resigned looking horses ate oats from buckets. Folk moiled setting up displays of items to sell. These folks looked like none he'd happened upon and he paused to study them more close-

ly. They seemed to belong to some sect or order pred-
icated on a system of restraints and deprivations. Their
clothing was made from dark cloth of a coarse weave and
all the men wore black flatcrowned hats and the women
black bonnets. Only the children looked at him. The children were altered in their manners as well and they stood
watching Yates watch the folk with the same frank curiosity, not like children at all but scaledown adults. The
men had luxuriant curling beards and blue clearlooking
eyes. Yates spoke to a man unloading willow baskets and
would have found out more about the order, but the man
just smiled at him and didn't answer, began sorting the
baskets by size into stacks in the shade of a walnut tree.

There was a girl about Yates's age who'd been watching him covertly from beneath the brim of her bonnet and
he smiled at her. She looked away.

You goin to be around here all day? he asked her.

She didn't say she was or she wasn't, but she gave
him a shy half smile then caught her lower lip between
her teeth and stood watching him. Her teeth were very
white.

Asha, the man with the baskets said brusquely. He
waited impatiently for her to help him. Then he came over
to Yates. We are very busy, he said.

I know how that is, Yates nodded. I'd be glad to give
you a hand with them baskets. He had a momentary vision of himself living with this sect. Wherever they lived.
The girl weaving baskets by the firelight, Yates doing
whatever the men did.

The man was shaking his head no. He was still smil-
ing but he seemed to be trying to hustle Yates on his way.

We have our own way, he said. We are simple.

I've been told that myself, Yates said, grinning
broadly, but the bearded man didn't see the humor in that,

or if he did, he did not acknowledge it. His hand clasped loosely on Yates's elbow.

We are simple, he repeated. We want no part of the world.

Yates jerked his arm away. I bet you'd sell it a basket though wouldn't ye? he asked. He went on up the street toward the middle of town. He glanced back quickly once and the girl called Asha was staring after him and the yellow dog was urinating on a wagonwheel.

At a restaurant called the Snowwhite Café, he drank a cup of coffee and ate two doughnuts. The doughnuts were rolled in powdered sugar and they were very good. He figured if he had access to them and the money to do so he'd eat one of them every day. He patted the sugar off his mouth with a napkin and took up his dishes and paid at the cash register and went out in the sun with a toothpick between his teeth. He was wishing there'd been someone here to see him. He wished Crowe had been here. To see him you would have thought he'd eaten in a restaurant thousands of times.

It had rained and the streets were muddy and rutted and crisscrossed with tracks from all manner of vehicles, wagons drawn by mules and buggies pulled by sleek-looking quarterhorses, mares highstepping delicately through the mud, and old highbacked trucks with flatbeds and sideboards cobbled out of sawmill slabs, and cars so crammed with folk you'd think if they all took a deep breath simultaneously the doors would spring open. The flatbeds and wagons all alighted with bigeyed kids who didn't know which wonder to look at first, all decked out bright as wildflowers in Sunday raiment and a blue haze of oilsmoke already shifting in the sunlight. There were sidewalk preachers tuning guitars with the box held against their ears to shut out the noise and a blind beggar

setting out his tin cup and a sign that said I AM JUST A
POOR COUNTRY BOY. Overall there was an almost feverish carnival air and Yates found himself caught up in it
and a core of excitement burned in the pit of his stomach
like banked embers.

Below the ice plant, in a lot grownup with hogweed and
thistle, a knot of men clustered about something Yates
couldn't see but he could hear their voices and occasional
raucous laughter and he figured as long as he was in town
he might as well take in as much as he could, so he sauntered toward the group. No one moved aside to let him
look too or even acknowledged his existence.

It took him a while to work his way toward the center
of the group and when he did he came upon a mudhole
with a rail pen built around it. In the mudhole was an alligator six or eight feet long. The alligator had fallen far
from any jungle splendor it might have known. Its knobby
moiled hide was slathered with drying black mud and it
was begarbed with foiled gumwrappers and bottlecaps.
It had clawed its way into the mud as fast as it could and
now it just lay with its strange clawed feet scratching its
hide occasionally to dislodge a steady onslaught of insects large and small and the drone of bottlegreen flies that
buzzed around it in a cloud. The alligator wore a leather
collar with a chain affixed and the chain was twisted into
muddy knots and the end of it was pinned to a steel stake
driven into the ground.

A grown boy of nineteen or so had a length of sawmill strip and he kept prodding the alligator through the

rails. The alligator seemed to be in the aftermath of some strenuous exertion, and it seemed to be resting. It ignored the prodding as best it could. Once when the stick prodded his jaws, he opened his mouth in a near soundless prolonged hiss that seemed curiously threatening. It clamped its jaws fast and just watched the stick contemptuously with its malignant little eyes.

Where'd it come from? he asked no one in particular.

Clyde Webb found it in his shithouse, a man said and several of the other men laughed. The big boy went on poking the alligator conscientiously as if poking alligators was what he did, and it was some job he'd been hired to do. Yates wondered if he ever tired, if perhaps they annoyed the alligator in shifts.

A young man in blue chambray and faded overalls gave him a cursory glance, then looked away past the clapboard and brick buildings toward where the town ended. There was the beginning of a wavering blue treeline. It came with that show, he said. That circus or whatever.

What's it eat?

An arm off clean to the elbow if you've a mind to feed it one, the man said.

Yates studied the alligator some more. It seemed to be asleep save that its dead little eyes were open. Yates turned to the boy with the stick.

Why do you keep stickin it like that? he asked.

The boy looked at him. What the hell is it to you? he asked.

Yates immediately wished he had said nothing at all.

The boy's face looked flat and unfriendly in the white weight of the sun. He had a curiously flattened nose as if it had been broken sometime in the past and improperly healed, as if it had been slammed flat against his face and just stayed there. He had a mouthful of rotten graylooking teeth and eyes as primitive and predatory as the alligator's.

It looks sick or somethin.

It didn't look so sick a few minutes ago when it was tryin to tear down that pen. What are you some kind of goddamned alligator doctor?

No, Yates said.

Where you from anyway? I don't know you and I know everbody.

I'm off of Allen's Creek, Yates said.

You're off all right, the boy said, or will be if you smartmouth me. I guess everbody off of Allen's Creek is an alligator expert. I guess you got em in springboxes down there.

Yates nodded. Yates was appalled at himself. He couldn't seem to help himself. He couldn't seem to shut up. We've had two or three ourselves, he said. We use em for watchdogs. I had one use to follow me to school in the morning and lay on the porch waiting for me. He got to where he knowed the bells and he'd take recess, was always waitin when school was let out. He was a smart alligator and it wouldn't surprise me none to know he learnt his ABCs.

You smartassed little prick.

Yates could feel icy sweat on his ribcage. His name was Spot, he heard himself say, but he finally took to runnin cars and the mailman run over him.

A few of the men sniggered.

The boy, or man, had relinquished all interest in the alligator and was studying Yates. His eyes measured him head to toe the way a professional might, a tailor, an undertaker. The way you'd measure a man for a suit of clothes, a coffin. He wore a winter shirt with the sleeves cut out and his bare arms were rawboned and muscled.

There was a sour reek of sweat about him.

You'll think one'd run over you when I'm through with you, he said. I've listened to all your mouth I aim to. I'm going to beat your sorry ass right in the mud.

Yates nodded. Likely you can, he said. But I ain't penned up. Or wearin no dog collar and chained to a post.

The man drew back somewhat, and Yates found himself in a circle of bodies facing the boy. The men waited like they were awaiting the commencing of some show. This seemed to serve as something that would help the time pass.

The man in the blue chambray shirt turned away from the fence. He dropped his homemade cigarette and toed it out in the dirt. Pug, he said.

What?

Leave him alone.

I will when I get through whippin his ass.

You're four or five years older than he is and a good foot taller. Let him be.

I aim to whip him.

Well, you won't do it here. Both of you go on about your business, if you've got any, and get the hell away from here.

Are you aimin to stop me?

I damn sure am, the man said. You've been stopped for a few minutes and you ain't even noticed it yet. I've knowed you all your life and watched you whup these old boys and kids don't want to fight you. You always know who to pick on and who not to. Think you're somethin of a fighter. Well I think it's about time you graduated. Stopped fightin boys and went to men. Folks is tired of it.

Are you jumpin in yourself, Bellwether? The man looked away, he seemed to have tired of the conversation.

I'm just tellin you how it is. You can take it any way

you want to.

The boy's eyes sidled away from Yates. I ain't done, he said. I'll get you when there ain't nobody around to protect you.

I can take care of myself, Yates said. Some invisible curtain seemed to have fallen.

Pug threw the sawmill stave toward the alligator, elbowed his way through the men. Whatever the show was seemed to be over. The men began to drift away as well. The blondehaired man in chambray leant against the rail fence.

I appreciate it, Yates told him.

I never done you any kindness. He'll do what he said. He'll lay for you, likely cold cock you with a rock from behind.

I can take care of myself.

Yeah, the man said.

He drifted down the midway awash in a haze of garish color and noise. Propelled along by throngs of other carnival goers, prematurely old farmers and their dry sour wives and stairstep children, young couples arm in arm and lost in each other and bands of running children roving in packs like predators. The smell of popcorn was everywhere and cotton candy and taffy apples, the swirling music of a calliope and, pitched below all this noise, the persistent cries of the barkers, grown desperate on this last night of the carnival and less discriminate as well, so even one as poorly endowed with worldly goods as Yates was besieged by their cries. To their eyes one fool no better than another.

He figured to see it all now that he was here. He was in no rush to see the cat. He kept it at the back of his mind like a promise he'd made himself. He paused at the end of the row of tents and looked up at the Ferris wheel. Perpetually faulted by the crisscrossing of insects, there was no sky, only a bright corona of blackness where the light ended. Against it the garish Ferris wheel tilting like a wheel spilling bright shards of laughter that fell all about Yates. Two girls holding hands watched the Ferris wheel. Their faces lacquered neon by the flickering colored lights. One had a heartshaped face haloed by dark hair. Watching Yates, she leant and whispered something in her companion's ear and they laughed.

He stood for a time before a tent set a little aside from the others and watched two brassy looking women in sequined swimsuits and peroxided hair dance about to raucous music that issued from somewhere inside the tent.

What you're seein here ain't nothin to what you'll see nude, a boredlooking barker cried into a megaphone. You'll see em take it all off and shake it for you and brother, they can shake it like a T-Model Ford driving across a plowed cornfield.

The women postured and leered and cupped their pendulous breasts and bounced their hips and hunched their pelvises at the gaping crowd of men. Yates noticed that one of them had flabby legs faultlined with a delicate tracery of varicose veins.

A few women straggled up in search of their men and some of them would take their sheepish looking men by the arm and lead them away grinning while others less successful stood in sullen silence as their men went into the hot darkness through the flap of the tent or they walked away toward the midway without looking back. Standing near the makeshift stage so as to miss nothing Yates was readily available and one of the women kissed him smearily on the jaw. I'd let this little cutie in for nothin, the blonde one said. Her lank blonde hair was as dead as if it had been electrocuted. She smelled of perfume and sweat.

Free was free and Yates wiped the lipstick off his jaw, started for the tent but the barker shook his head no and the women broke into raucous laughter. After a time, and with no signal Yates was privy to, it was time for the show and the women jounced toward the tent and the barker went into a last minute frenzied spiel and began to collect money from the men. Yates stood for a time with the spurned wives listening to the sounds from the tent and then he went back onto the midway.

He came upon the girl with the pale heartshaped face. She was divested of her companion and Yates's hand counted coins in his pocket. You want to ride that Ferris wheel? he asked. She did. She wanted cotton candy too and he bought that. They rode with her clasping the paper cone of spun sugar carefully before her like something of great value that might be arrested from her. He was surprised at the abrupt onset of flight when the wheel started, and again when it stopped with a creaking sway of the seats to take on more riders, higher still till he involuntarily clasped her hand and thought his breath would explode in his chest. Below them the widening world was lost in a phantasmagoria of light.

The girl rode beside him in a calm companionable silence. Yates's mind was in a seething turmoil. Her sweet face against the yellow shifting haze, newly minted and bright and perfect as anything that ever was. His mind striving to concoct so vast a lie that she would instantly love him without question, would follow him anywhere.

When the ride was over and they stood a moment

waiting for their legs to get accustomed to the solidity of earth the girl was scooped up by an angryfaced woman and led away. The girl waved at him, the other hand still clutching the cotton candy.

Where do you live? he called, but she only turned and grinned and mouthed, In a house.

He had to ask four or five people about the cat before he found the animals. No one seemed to know anything about a cat. He could have found the pen by the smell alone but there was no cat that he could find. There was a great gray mottled elephant tied to a chinaberry tree and its bored looking trainer attendant. Yates unfolded the worn foolscap handbill and showed it to the carny. I don't know nothin about it, the carny said. I been here awhile and I ain't seen one. We got a hippo all the way from Africa though, he gestured. Yates looked toward the heavy gauge chainlinked fence the hippo was caged in. I don't care nothin about no hippo, he said contemptuously.

The hippo was huge and ugly and graceless, dirty and its hide crept with vermin, nothing like the sleek free and perhaps ultimately uncageable cat he had dreamed of and hoboed from Allen's Creek to see. He was storing up this vast world of data indiscriminately, who knew what would be valuable. Someone who'd never seen one might want a hippo described to them.

Nobody's makin you look at her, the carny said. You can look or let her be.

It just looks like a hog to me, he said. We got hogs on Allen's Creek. I never jumped on no movin boxcar train and rode all this way to see some overgrown hog.

He went to look anyway, crowding his way into a throng of people studying this strange beast who'd wandered so far from home. It stood ankledeep in muddy straw with its back toward Yates, glancing once back over its shoulder at him. Its piggy little eyes looked bright with malice, as if perhaps it held Yates and Yates alone responsible for its confinement.

Yates could feel people jostling about him, their weight forcing him against the wire net. You ever seen anything like that, boy? an old man said excitedly into his ear, but Yates just gave him a withering glance and didn't reply. He was wondering where they might keep the cat and whether it might cost more to see it when the hippo leant slightly forward, its feet spread, hunching its shoulders. Others perhaps more worldly to the ways of hippos stepped ostensibly back or to the side away from the chainlink fence leaving Yates alone leant against it and Yates was suddenly inundated in a hot stream of foulsmelling urine so hard he staggered backward and fell under the onslaught of this loathsome yellow rain, then staggered up unbelieving with a strangled cry of rage.

People were laughing hysterically, pointing, clapping each other on the back. A motley convention of longlost brothers. One man was hanging onto the chinaberry tree in a choking gale of laughter.

You son of a bitch, Yates said. He wished for a gun, a rock, a rusty spoon, anything. He was soaked and reeking and his feet squished wetly when he moved. He advanced on the hippo unarmed and barehanded and had to be hauled fighting down from the chainlink fence by the carny. Folks with tearstained faces had turned back toward the cage thinking there may be a second act to this show but the carny made shoving motions with his hands. You all get on away from here and leave the boy alone, he said. It ain't nothin to laugh about. Then he got a good look at Yates and his face twisted and he turned away clutching his sides. Somebody's fixin to pay for this, Yates said. He started back toward the midway.

The man sidling Yates between the darkened tents had none of the exotic touches Yates had expected. Neither in speech nor in appearance. In fact, he might have come out of a backwoods similar to the one Yates had come from an inch at a time or yet in some curious and almost occult way the selfsame woods a few years earlier.

In here, the man said, holding aside the flap of the tent. Yellow lanternlight. A man sat at a folding table drinking from a cutglass goblet what appeared to be wine. The man was dark, and as exotic as Yates might have hoped for. He may have been black, but his hair was straight and pulled back over his shoulder into a ponytail. In the shadows of a corner was a cot, a young woman seated upon it held a child. It fed at her dark breast. Yates found himself fighting not to look.

The man watched Yates with large dark liquidlooking eyes. Well, well, he said. What have we here?

He wants his money back, he said.

Say he does? We have a longstanding policy of no refunds, Leonard. You know that by now.

Well, he won't leave. He's telling folks it's all a gyp. He had an accident with the hippo, the carny said.

I guess there's a first time for everything, the owner said. What kind of an accident? Was the hippo not a beast?

The man beside Yates grinned and turned his face away. The hippo's fine, he said.

Yates was almost incandescent with rage. I came here to see a panther, he said. A black panther. I seen it on one of your showcards. I come a long way and paid good money and aim to see it.

I told him there ain't no panther, the young carny said.

I seen the picture, Yates said.

Leonard is right. Indeed, there is no panther, the owner said. The panther died. It was old and it got sick and one morning it was dead in its cage and it was just gone. There's no panther.

You ought to have said ahead of time, Yates said. It was an effort to control his voice.

The man sighed. We have other animals, he said. We have more animals than we do complaints. Nowhere in our advertising do we specifically say we have a panther. But I want to hear more about this hippo thing. What kind of an accident with the hippopotamus?

Yates glanced at the woman. She seemed to feel a nigh imperceptible weight of his glance and he saw that her face was smooth and impenetrable as the opaque side of one way glass. I hate to say, Yates said.

Go ahead, the man told him. We're old friends here.

Yates took a breath. Anger seized him anew and his voice shook. All right, he said, all right. I come here all the way from Allen's Creek on a train to see that cat. There ain't no cat. I was lookin at this hippo thing right close and, all at once, it pissed on me. It pissed on me a lot. My clothes is wet and my shoes is full of it and I smell so bad folks crosses to get out of my way. I want my money. I just want it over with, I want my money back or I want to see the panther.

The panther died, the man said again.

I know a hippopotamus that's in danger of the very same thing, Yates said.

Perhaps it took a liking to you, the man said. It's common knowledge that in the world of hippos that's a gesture of affection.

Yates spat onto the straw floor of the tent. He seemed to find this unworthy of comment and he made none.

The man sighed again. Oh hell, he said. We can't satisfy everybody. He withdrew his sheaf of folded bills from the inside of his breast pocket. He unsheathed a worn dollar bill and laid it on the card table and smoothed it with his fingers, here you are, he said. A fourfold return on your money. That ought to make up for your various inconveniences.

There ain't enough money in the world to make me let that crazy thing piss on me again, Yates said, but he picked up the money angrily. He pocketed the money and went out without walking back onto the midway. He went through the throng of folks with stunned and weary faces. From the tent behind he heard laughter, real or imagined, and bright with anger he passed on into the starblown night.

He awoke in a sour miasma of dread with the weight of the midmorning sun on his eyelids. When he opened his eyes all he could see was the pulsing yellow furnace of the sun glaring out of an electric blue sky. He closed them. His lids felt sunburned. He was lying on his back atop a tie pile and little by little he became aware of the hard wood beneath him, a foul stench rank with animal musk, as if he'd fallen asleep in an animal's lair. Awareness seeped in. Goddamn it's me, he said aloud. He arose and climbed down off the tie pile. The smell was rising off him in almost invisible waves.

He looked toward the town. It baked in the sun, no one in sight, through the vibratory heat waves rising from the railroad tracks, it lay in Sunday quietude. Against the fierce blue sky it looked vaguely unreal, a mockup town for some drama not yet staged, or one that happened long ago. A strong wind would likely tilt it over, you'd see beyond it, the vibratory summer trees and the muddy river uncoiling in the sun.

He struck off toward the railroad tracks, followed them toward the town until he came upon a big yellow clapboard building. Over the single door a sign said: Depot, but a closed sign hung on the door. There was no one about. Well, hell, he said. He walked over to the railroad tracks and looked down them in the direction he had come. They curved away to vaguely gleaming invisibility. Beyond them, all there was of the wide world's turning was hammered sky and a shimmering treeline. He stood for a time uncertainly peering down the tracks like a man waiting for a scheduled train. He didn't know if the depot was closed all day on Sunday and he didn't know if trains ran when depots closed. He didn't know much at all except that it was a long way to Allen's Creek and that he was enormously thirsty.

There was a bent spigot sprouting like some mutant weed out of the packed gravel bed the little depot was set on and Yates turned it on. A thin gout of rustcolored water trickled forth, dwindled to nothing and ceased. He kicked it impotently a time or two but he couldn't make it work. He turned and walked listlessly toward the settlement. He was looking for anywhere water might be. He went through the business section of town such as it was and up into a residential section where great white houses crouched brooding over the river. Everywhere a lush air of melancholy leisure.

The only soul he saw was a grizzled old black man watering an enormous lawn. The cropped green grass climbed steeply upward toward a faded mansion, columns, screened in porches, some rich man's house, a remnant of faded grandeur. He stood for a time watching the fanning spray of water but the colored man didn't acknowledge him. A small rainbow gleamed through a prism of spray.

I need me a drink, Yates finally said.

The old man glanced at him. Then gave him a thorough measured inspection up and down. He seemed not to know what to make of this foulsmelling apparition.

It ain't nothin but water, he finally said at length.

I ain't such a fool I have to be told what comes out of a hosepipe, Yates said. Can I have a drink or not?

The old man wordlessly handed him the hose. Yates drank deeply, feeling the cold water ballooning in his belly. The old man was already reaching a clawed hand for the hose, glancing nervously up the hill toward the house.

Yates held the hose over his head, letting the water cascade out of his hair in dirty rivulets, washing himself onehanded like a cat. Here, here, the old man kept saying impatiently. He kept trying to wrest the hose away from Yates and Yates kept holding it out of his reach and letting water spray over them both until the old man backpedaled out of range and yelled at him.

You wastin Mr. Tookie's water, he screamed. I never said you could take no shower bath.

Yates handed him the hose. Well hell take it, he said. I never knowed it was rationed or nothin.

The old man grasped the hose possessively. He began to water wildly, hurrying as if he had to make up for lost time. Mr. Tookie couldn't pay the water bill for what water it'd take to clean you up and him a wealthy man. You told me you wanted a drink. It's a whole river out there for bathin.

Why hell yes, Yates said, the Tennessee River. I don't know why I never thought about the river.

He could smell the river before he saw it, a damp rich

pungent smell of earth, fish, some primeval undercurrent he couldn't put a name to. He kept clear of the houses and approached the river through a stand of willows, following a worn path down a packed clay embankment encysted with popbottle caps to a little grove of cypress, a sandy spit of beach that ran out into the water. The cypresses gave him a measure of privacy and the sand was white and clean.

Why hellfire, he said. I ought to been here all the time. A man could set up housekeeping in a place like this and me sleepin on a tiepile.

He shucked out of his clothes and waded thighdeep into the tepid water feeling its warm sensuous movement against his legs. He went on deeper until it pressed against his throat like warm gentle hands, his feet shifting on the muddy bottom. Far across the river, rolling green farms and red barns drifted in an unreal haze, a calendar scene, a scene of plenty, a misty pastoral dream.

He staggered out with the mud sucking at his feet and stood shivering in the sun on the sandbar but he could still smell himself. He went kneedeep into the river and scrubbed himself with handfuls of sand. I bet I'm the only person in this round world scrubbin hippopotamus piss off hisself this mornin, he thought.

After he'd bathed he started to dress himself but it seemed pointless to put the fouled clothes back on so he dipped them in the river and wallowed them around and scrubbed them until he couldn't smell them anymore. Then he put on the dripping trousers and hung the shirt to dry on a cypress branch and seated himself on a rock in the sun for the pants to dry and just stared at the shimmering river.

After awhile he heard something like a train whistle far up the river and watched intently until finally a string of barges hove into view rounding the curve. There were eight of them lashed together in some fashion and they rode low in the water, heaped with what appeared to be mountains of coal. They were going downriver with the current and the tug pushed them almost effortlessly. Men lounged against the rails and watched the country slip past. Yates raised a hand in greeting and a black man on the tug returned it solemnly and the procession passed on soberly as a funeral train freighting its cargo of dead to a shore lost in mist. He watched it far downriver, the tug's horn growing faint and finally lost.

Before his clothing was dry he heard voices and laughter then footfalls on the path, but before he hid, three small black children came onto the beach with fishing poles and a bucket of bait. When they saw Yates their laughter immediately ceased. They veered back into the scrub as if they'd flee him.

Hey, you all go ahead and fish, Yates said. I ain't aimin to bother you. It ain't my river nohow.

They came back onto the sandspit warily as if they were prepared for instant flight should Yates leap upon them or begin to wave a gun about. The oldest boy looked to be about thirteen and when he set the baitbucket down and began to feel about in it the other two followed suit.

Ain't you fishin here?

Naw. I ain't even got a pole. I just been in there swimming.

Cottonmouth bite you on the pecker, one of the younger boys grinned slyly.

They snakes in here?

They mostly in the sloughs, the older boy said. He's just foolin with you. They was cottonmouth in here you'd not catch me here. I had a buddy was bit by three of em in a slough and they never even got him to the doctor. Could have just took him on to the graveyard.

What you catch, anything?

The boy had baited his hook with a redworm and seated himself on a rock by the river's edge. He spat on the worm. He adjusted the cork float and flung the line into the river.

We catches a few. Carps mostly. Few little channel cats. They's catfish in here biggern a man but they stays in the deep water.

Does the place shut down entirely on a Sunday? Ain't no stores or nothin open up in town?

It's a little grocer store I think open up after dinner. A cabstand.

A cabstand? I don't reckon I could afford a cab to Allen's Creek. I wouldn't think they'd be enough business to keep a cabstand runnin in a little place like this.

They sells whiskey on the side. Folks plays cards there.

I don't reckon I need any of that either but there might be somebody there knows something bout the trains. I need to catch me a train to Allen's Creek. You don't know anything about when the train run do you?

The boy shook his head. They just run now and again. Whenever they've a mind to I reckon. He fell silent, studying the hammered surface of the river. I wished I had me a boat. I had me a boat of some kind I'd catch me one of them six foot catfish and sell it off by the pound. That put me on easy street.

In the early afternoon he counted the remainder of his change and ventured uptown wandering around until he found the grocerystore, a tiny crackerbox store like a child's mockup of a store with a few overpriced groceries aimed at the black trade. He bought bologna and bread and cakes and a Coca-Cola and when he paid up he had three copper pennies left. Swinging the bag along he went down a steep winding backstreet toward the river and came upon the cabstand. Its plateglass window said Helton's Dry Cleaner, but someone had painted through it and written deVries Cab Company beneath it. The window had been broken and patched by an elaborate spiderweb of masking tape, and it was slightly concave and had a fragile look to it.

Inside was a long narrow room, cool and dark and cavernous. A fan whirred somewhere overhead moving the layers of smoke about. The only light came from the rear where a suspended fluorescent light illuminated a pool table with the bright cold clarity of a green baize autopsy table. Yates stood for a moment blinking and letting his eyes adjust to the gloom. Two figures like shadow men moved ritualistically about the table. The soft click of pool balls, the murmur of voices.

What could I do for you?

He turned. A short ratfaced man was watching him from behind a long counter.

Do what?

I figured this bein a cabstand you might need one.

No I just been wanderin around town tryin to find out something about the trains. How often they run trains out of this place anyhow?

The man looked all about. Walls, floor, ceiling.

They ain't never run none out of here that I know of and I been here ten years.

Hellfire. You know what I mean. I mean out of Akerman's Field. You know anything about when they run?

I don't keep no railroad timetables. I'll run a cab

though anytime you pay me to.

I need to go all the way to Allen's Creek. I reckon I'll wait on a train goin that way.

The man shrugged. Well, he said, I don't run no trains.

A long row of benches ran the length of the room. Sepia images of folk appearing out of the serried gloom. Old overalled men, young bucks in their town clothes. One young man with something strangely familiar about him was studying Yates with grim appraisal. He grinned, a gaptoothed pumpkin, and when he did Yates recognized him. The way the sun had struck his flattened face when he'd leant to prod the alligator with the sawmill stave. Shitfire, Yates thought. Where do all these sons of a bitches come from?

He went out hearing behind him the creak of the bench then footsteps. The door open and close. He sauntered casually up the street. Halfway up the block he looked back. Pug was sauntering along behind, elaborately casual, whistling, hands in pockets. He quickened his pace, glanced over his shoulder. Pug wasn't even looking but he had begun walking faster. He seemed lost in study of old brick buildings crowding the narrow street. Faster still. By the time he crested the hill Yates was fairly running, and from the flat steps of shoes behind him he knew Pug was running too.

When he came onto the street of the hill's summit onto the square he went right and through a ruined doorway that opened only into the shell of a building with high crumbling brick walls on all four sides. The old brick crept with poisonoak, the paved floor was cracked and grown with weeds, and an ancient greaserack sat frozen in the air like an arcane altar. The ground strewn with old greaseblack motors and transmissions and odd wheels.

He was looking all about, but save scaling the high brick walls there was no way out. He dropped the bag he was carrying, stepped to the side when he heard running footsteps. He could feel the wall hard against his back. Pug came fulltilt through the doorway and ran to the center of the building windmilling his arms to stop his flight, looking wildly about and, when he ultimately turned, he saw Yates was blocking the doorway and he had the open knife clinched in his fist.

Momentary confusion flickered and died on Pug's face. You wouldn't cut me, he said.

Not unless I can get within reach, Yates said.

It better have chocolate handles, Pug said, because I mean to make you eat the son of a bitch.

He took two steps forward, crouched, feign to go left or right should Pug try to get around him. Pug stood his ground. His eyes were flickering all about for something to serve as a weapon but there didn't seem to be anything light enough to pick up.

I'm twice your size. Hell that knife weighs you sideways. You think I can't just take it away from you.

I doubt you can. That is unless you don't care what shape you're in when you do get it. You think I'm just goin to stand here while you take it? You think I'm goin to shut the blade and just lay it in your hand?

I don't think you've got the hair on your ass to cut me. You know too well what'd happen next. Ain't no Bellwether here to hold your hand this time.

Yates was seized by an uncontrollable rage. He felt frozen and feverish. Words he couldn't control tumbled out of him.

I'm sick of all of you crazy son of a bitches, Yates said. I never bothered you today and I never bothered you yesterday. I reckon everybody in this pissant town thinks he's a smartass. I've been lied to, made fun of and laughed at and pissed on by wild animals and everybody I meet wants to whip my ass. When I pass the city limits I'll never look back. I been to this place twice, my first time and my last.

You ain't out of it yet and ain't likely to be. What of you ain't eat by the catfishes likely float out.

Then come ahead. You'll be totin your dick in your pocket for a rabbit's foot before I'm through with you. Come on, if you're as dirt ignorant as you look like you are.

I ain't got no knife and you're just crazy enough to do it.

I damn sure am.

All right then get the fuck out of here. I'll let you off this time. I ain't gettin my stomach cut just to whip your ass. Hell, they ain't nothing to you but mouth and pocketknife. Go on. Git about your business.

It ain't that easy, Yates said. I believe I'll just cut you anyway. I'm sick of your mouth. I'm sick of having to look over my shoulder all the time just to see what's following me. I believe I'll just kill you and be done with you once and for all.

He was breathing hard. He looked down at the knife. The knuckles were bone white on his clenched fist. He could feel sweat running down his ribcage and into the waistband of his jeans. He went over by the doorway and seated himself on a concrete block. His knees were shaking and he couldn't make them quit. Sweat was running out of his hair and into his eyes. He wiped it away with the back of his free hand. Through his perspiration blurred vision he could see Pug hadn't moved.

You go on yourself, Yates said. Git on about your business. I don't care what you do. Tell em you whipped my ass or whatever. But just leave me alone. Next time it'll be me laying for you and I can fix it so nobody'd ever know what happened to you. I doubt you'd be missed anyway.

Pug moved jerkily forward. A marionette at the hands of an unskilled puppeteer. He skirted the knife and went through the door sideways.

You're crazy as a shithouse mouse, he said.

Yates didn't deny it. He sat on the concrete block with the knife clenched between his knees. He sat for a time breathing slowly and deeply and then he took up the bag his supper was in and went out. He halfexpected Pug to leap upon him but Pug was nowhere to be seen. He went on waiting for flung stones to strike him in the head or between the shoulder blades but that never happened either.

That night on the river he slept and woke and slept fitfully again. In the dark of the night a dream of trains woke him. He was awake and sitting upright when he heard the whistle of a tug with a string of barges resplendent with light and through the river fog their voice came to him disjointed and disorienting like remnants of a dream or fragments of a conversation he wasn't meant to hear. The barges seemed some enormous lost city dislodged from the very solidity of earth itself and bejeweled with light, drifting irrevocably lost toward the rim of the world.

Here and there, up and down the riverbanks, flares of the fires of campers and their voices came sourceless and strange, a world of unconnected words meant for other ears than his own. He heard soft meaningless feminine laughter, the chords of a guitar. He'd a fire of his own he'd built not for the heat, but for illusion of companionship and now he rebuilt it, stacking crosswise thin branches of grassy pine. The fire caught, sparks cascaded upward and lost.

At first light birds called him awake where he slept on the riverbank, a veritable madhouse of caws and chirps and twittering that began with the advent of day and increased with the encroaching light. He struggled against waking as if the day held more than he could handle and he wanted no part of it. He'd fallen asleep in some curious aviary walled only by the trees and when the cries grew more strident and persistent, he discarded his strange dreams and sat looking out across the river. There was no commerce on it as yet and the surface was calm, as warped and wonkylooking as distressed sheet metal. Far across in distant haze the other shore looked new and unspoiled. There was no trace of man or his works and the countryside looked like the shore of some vague and lovely world only rumored, not yet tainted by civilization.

He arose and made ready to go, glancing about once like a man checking out of a hotel room looking to see has he forgotten anything. He had not. There was nothing to take into the day save Yates and the clothes on his back. He struck out up the riverbank. Curious little town built on hills. Winding precipitous sidestreets, you seemed always to be climbing or descending stairsteps.

He came upon the main drag where folk were beginning to mill purposefully about, then veered south through a warren of shacks clinging to hillsides with parched looking nighvertical gardens attendant with nothing he recognized and through backyards strung with clotheslines where hung ragged graylooking clothes and through front yards past silent watchdogs on tangled chains. No one seemed up save some old grandmother warming in the sun who did not acknowledge his existence. He seemed to move through here in furtive invisibility. Begarbed shacks halfpainted as if their tenants had given up and thrown the brushes away, blownout automobiles deceased and stripped of their viable organs, some already buried in honeysuckle and kudzu. He moved through a land locked in silence, a place that seemed to be reeling in the aftershock of some cataclysm that had come in the night and whose impact had not yet been assessed. He quickened his steps.

He came out near the railroad tracks four or five blocks up from the depot. He went past a sprawling clapboard building that had been remodeled and added onto endlessly as if constructed by carpenters who could come to no sort of agreement as to what they were building. It moved backward in a series of diminishing rooflines and the last addition seemed designed for littlefolk or leprechauns, so near the ground it was. There was a red Diamond-T truck backed to the front porch and a heavyset man was loading blocks of ice onto it with a set of tongs. Another man sat leaning against a porch stanchion with his face in his hands. He seemed to be grieving. Yates had seen this truck before or one like it and he went closer to inspect it. When he turned his attention back to the seated man he saw that he was holding crushed ice in his cupped palms and he was rubbing his face with it.

The man with the tongs slammed a fifty-pound block of ice onto the bed of the truck and stepped back to the porch.

You better get to coverin this shit up, he told the seated man. I get paid to sell it and that's all and here I am loading it. But I'll be damned if I'm covering it and everything else.

The man lowered his palms and looked at the melting ice and rubbed it into his sparse gray hair. Chunks of ice lay there and began to melt and the cold water ran down his forehead. His eyes were fey looking and drunken, one with a rightward cast as if it would have a wider vision of the world or at the very least a different perspective on it.

I was tryin to remember where I stayed last night, the man said. It's right on the edge of my mind but I just can't get hold of it. I wish I could. Seems like I done somethin awful or somebody done somethin awful to me but I'll be damned if I can remember what. I wish I could just remember where I stayed.

Where was you when you woke up? Yates asked, becoming interested in this mystery in spite of himself. That always seems to help me. Generally, where I wake up is about where I fell asleep at.

The man looked at him and then he looked away. He shook his head and didn't say anything.

Where was your truck at when you woke up?

The man studied Yates without expression, with a face that bore him no animosity that perhaps welcomed the rationalizations of a logical mind.

Ahh, he said. My truck. My truck was here, where I left it yesterday when the ice plant was closed. I can keep up with my truck. It's me I keep losin.

None of this is gettin ice loaded and covered up, the man with the tongs said.

Ain't I seen you on Allen's Creek? Who are you?

I'm the iceman, the man said. You liable to see me most anywhere. I'm the iceman, he sang in a tuneless crooning. I'm the iceman, the iceman, better get out of my way.

Yates turned to go.

Hey, the man said. Yates stopped.

I'll give you two dollars if you'll get that scoop and sawdust the ice down. Cover it over and put the tarps over it.

Yates looked at the size of the truck. The ice stacked in its bed. The mounded pile of sawdust.

I already got two dollars, he said.

All right, I'll give you four. Hellfire, ain't you got no ambition? Here I am offerin you double, I say double your worldly goods for a few minutes work and you don't even want to hear it. What's the matter with these young folks today?

Where you takin this ice?

The iceman studied. Monday, he told himself. He looked at Yates. I'm goin out Riverside and up Allen's Creek. Back through Oak Grove.

I'll do it if you throw in a ride to Allen's Creek.

The man stuck out a hand and Yates shook it. The hand was wet and cold as ice, just the way an iceman's hand should be, Yates thought.

He took up the scoop and the man with the tongs showed him what to do. The blocks of ice were spaced two or three inches apart and Yates carefully filled in between them with sawdust and between the ice and the sideboards. When that was done, a layer thrown loosely over it all, the man with the tongs began to stack more ice. A layer of ice, a layer of sawdust. At last the man signaled he was through and Yates covered the last layer and drew the tarp over it and lashed it down.

The iceman was up and about and with enormous effort he opened the truck door and climbed in. Yates got in the other side.

You have to hold onto that handle, the iceman said. Door'll fly open on a curve and sail your skinny ass down a hillside.

Yates sat clutching the door handle bothhanded. The iceman was staring out the windshield.

Well now, he said. He was looking at the world with intense concentration, as if it were coming at him at a hundred miles an hour and he was charged with negotiating its curves and byways. He reached out and turned the ignition and the truck coughed into life and set idling. He nodded. All right, all you unrefrigerated sons of bitches, he said. Here comes the iceman.

Four or five miles out of town they went through a flatlands where the road paralleled the river and Yates could see not the river itself but the upper half of a barge that seemed to be cruising by some miraculous locomotion through willows and a stand of sassafras. Then the road curved upward into the hills and he could smell hot piney woods baking in the sun, astringent and somehow nostalgic.

The iceman at first drove with the exaggerated care of a drunk who doesn't quite trust himself. As his confidence grew and the pitch to the motor wound higher he began to croon mindlessly to himself. The iceman, here comes the iceman, better get out of my way.

He walled his off eye up at Yates. You ever been so drunk you couldn't remember where you was or what you done?

Lord no, Yates said, clinging religiously to the door handle. I can barely find my way through a day cold sober. I'd not even attempt one drunk.

I never could make much sense of it drunk or sober, the iceman said. Seems like it just went easier drunk though.

Yates didn't reply. The road had climbed into terrain near mountainous that he was wary of and the road was snaking around narrow switchback curves. The one eye kept glancing at Yates and Yates wished it would watch the road. The truck kept rounding curves on the blind side and Yates was watching them apprehensively. Red rock climbed sheer on the left and looking down from his window he could see the earth dropping away in a manner that took his breath away and he tightened his grip on the door handle as if in some talismanic way it was holding the truck on the road.

It's in like a dark place, the iceman said. I can almost see in there but whatever's in there slips back out of sight. Sometimes I nearly think of it and then it's gone.

Godalmighty, Yates said.

They'd rounded a leftleaning curve on the wrong side and two enormous black mules were suddenly upon them, the left mule rearing with wild rolling eyes and its hoofs slamming onto the hood then its head turning against the actual glass with whitewalled eyes frantic then gone and the wagon with the old man's face a rictus of absolute horror and him trying to whip the mules onto an impossible course, sawing the lines and cutting them into the sheer wall with the wagon tilting and the iron rims sparking against the granite bluff. The truck struck the left rear wheel of the wagon and carried it away with the wagon turning and sliding crosswise behind them, Yates whirling watching through the back glass the overalled man spilled from the wagonbed then whirling back to see coming at him across the hood a frieze of rock and greenery clockwise in such elongation the landscape seemed stretched to transparency as the brakelocked truck swapped ends in the gravel and the horizon itself fleeing vertically downward as the truck tilted backward off the shoulder of the road and the truck cab filled with intense blue sky.

The iceman was humming crazily to himself. He'd locked the brakes and when he released them the truck accelerated backward down the hill with him watching out the windshield trees that seemed to come from nowhere fleeing backward, brush that sprang erect from beneath them like imaged brush in a pop-up book, him giving the steering wheel little meaningless cuts right or left. He seemed not to know where he was.

Hit the goddamned brakes, Yates screamed. Yates was peering out the back glass, at once trying to see where they were going and fearful of it.

When the iceman slammed the brakes the motor stalled and died and the load of ice shot backward down the slope, disappearing off the bed like a frozen waterfall then the truck lurching and jouncing across it and the ice reappearing magically before them, great chunks strewn like gleaming hailstones from a storm of unreckonable magnitude.

Cut it into a tree, Yates yelled, but before he'd even finished saying it the truck slammed into a treetrunk so hard the force of it whipped his head into the back glass then forward into the windshield. They sat in a ringing appalled silence, Yates clutching his head, the iceman staring up the hillside the way they'd come. Outraged crumpled saplings, crushed cedars, ice everywhere.

All them folks, the iceman said.

Do what? Yates asked. He thought the iceman was talking about the collision with the wagon and he'd only seen one man.

All them folks waitin on me. With their hot jugs of

tea. Their ice cream freezers. Where's the iceman, they'll say. He ain't never been this late before.

Yates was shaking and he couldn't stop. You are absolutely the craziest shitass in the whole history of the world, he said.

The iceman was trying to get his door open. It seemed to be stuck, jammed where it struck the wagon wheel. At length he turned in the seat and kicked it hard bothfooted and it sprang open.

Help me, he said. We got to get that ice gathered up.

I wish I had sense like other folks, Yates said. I'd be better off in hell with my back broke than ever crawlin in a truck with you.

I got money tied up in this ice. Help me reload and we'll scotch this truck somehow and I'll try to drive us out.

Yates looked. He was shaking his head.

You couldn't drive up that bluff in a goddamned Army tank, he said. She ever comes out of here she'll have a block and tackle tied to her.

Nevertheless, it's got to be done, the iceman said. He staggered up the slope clutching to saplings. Yates clambered out of the canted truck cab. It was hard even to stand here, so precipitous and undependable was the earth. He looked down on a fairyland of treetops, a tiny pink road winding somewhere. He sat down and began to inspect himself for wounds.

The iceman had selected a fifty-pound block of ice. He was stumbling toward the truck with it clutched before him like some offering he was making. Suddenly he halted stockstill as if the ice had frozen him in his tracks. He had a peculiar look on his face.

Son of a bitch, he said.

What?

A dance, the iceman said. He sat the ice down carefully then seated himself upon it. Elbows on knees, hands clasped before him. He seemed to be in deep thought.

What?

I killed somebody, the iceman said.

Who? Yates was thinking about the wagon, the man sliding roadward.

Some girl, the iceman said. Some woman. We was at a dance. One of them beerjoints down by the river. I don't even remember what we got into it about. I took to beatin her with somethin ... seems like it was a singletree but I don't know where in the shit I'd get a singletree. A stick maybe. A big stick. I remember she kept tryin to crawl off into the bushes. I kept hitting her and hitting her.

Yates was watching him apprehensively. He could feel ice water tracking down his rib cage. He glanced upward to the rim of the earth where the road ran, figuring perhaps angles of inclination, speed when fleeing madmen.

Maybe you just slapped her around a little, he said hopefully.

The iceman thought about it a while. He took a package of Camel cigarettes from a shirt pocket and tipped one out and just sat holding it. His hands were wet from the ice and after a time it shredded in his fingers.

No, he finally said. He shook his head. No. I killed her all right. She was all busted up and limber. I remember rakin wet black leaves over her face.

Yates arose. He dusted off the seat of his jeans.

I got to get on, he said. It's a long way to Allen's Creek.

The iceman appeared not to hear. Yates climbed a few feet up the slope and then he turned. I need to get that money, he said.

What money?

That four dollars for loading the truck.

The iceman fumbled out a wallet, sat studying its contents.

I'd double it again if you'd help me reload.

I got to get on.

The iceman carefully counted off four one dollar bills, rubbing each one carefully between thumb and forefinger. Yates took the proffered money and pocketed it.

Appreciate it, he said.

Anytime, the iceman said. You want to help me as a regular thing, the job's open.

Yates didn't reply. When he was halfway up the hillside he looked down. The iceman had risen and he had begun to gather the blocks of ice and restack the truck. Yates went on. The next time he looked back the iceman raised a hand in a curiously formal gesture, farewell, and Yates raised an arm, farewell, and clambered onto the road.

He stood breathing hard. Far down the winding road the farmer appeared riding a mule. The wagon and the other mule were nowhere in sight.

He turned. Beyond the rim the world lay in a crazyquilt patchwork of soft pastel fields, tracts of somber woods. Folded horizons so far in the distance they trembled and veered in the heat and ultimately vanished. Somewhere in that dreammist lay Allen's Creek. He'd have traded a year of his life for a handful of its dust. He spat and wiped the sweat out of his eyes and struck out toward it.

BOOK III

HARRIKIN

Now that he was back in town, Yates longed to see Cassie.

When she could come out it would be far after midnight and they would climb Paiton Hill for what little breeze there was and he'd lie on the cool rails with the steel cool against his spine and the sweet distillation of honeysuckle heady as a drug. Cold spill of stars so close he fancied he could touch them.

Thanks for slippin out, he said. I know you'd be in trouble if she caught you.

Well, she said lightly, trouble is what I know best.

He could see the shape of her dress. Her pale arms laced across paler knees. He knew with a weight in his heart that he'd never see anything he thought lovelier.

Still I'm glad you did.

Well, when you consider the alternative, you're not so bad.

Do what?

The alternative. A bunch of old drunks trying to grab your titties.

Emboldened he said: I wouldn't mind grabbin one or two of them myself, then decided that didn't quite sound right.

I'd think you saw enough the first time I saw you.

I couldn't see em enough if I lived to be a hundred years old. Besides I never even seen em. I was too busy tryin to git rid of Lillie.

Oh, quit it you fool.

I paid high dollar for that. I got beltbuckle scars on my back on account of the lies that old bat told on me. Not to mention I'm livin here and there like a haint. Livin without walls and sleep wherever night overtakes me.

Granny doesn't like you very much.

Doesn't like me? Well, no she don't. She hates me like a mad dog hates water. She's always hated me and I ain't too damn fond of her.

She don't care what I do as long as I don't do it with you. She said you stole a goat from her and hit her with a shovel. Did you?

Yes, I did.

Why on earth would you do that?

It was my goat died and I stole it to bury it. I don't count that stealin it. I couldn't stand the thought of her eatin it. I did hit her with a shovel, I meant to kill her but my aim was off. If I'd had a gun Allen's Creek would been short one bootlegger.

You ever think about what might have been? And if you'd killed her we never would have met. If you hadn't stolen that goat and hit her with a shovel we might be courting in Granny Stovall's parlor. You could bring me a bouquet of honeysuckles and a sack of candy from Dow's and we could sit on the couch and plan our wedding. Lillie Mae would be my bridesmaid.

Black Crowe would have to be my best man, he said. Crowe may be a nigger but he's the only friend I got in this wide world. Or any other.

Granny could give us the attic room and you wouldn't have to live like a haint anymore. I could sew buttons on your shirts and Lillie Mae could knit you stockings. In the wintertime, a scarf.

He had wearied of the games. He wasn't good at them and she was and anyway, games were not what he was here for.

Anyway, who's this Thomas Wolfe you love to talk about? Some boy you knew in Alabama?

Oh Lord. Thomas Wolfe is a writer, he wrote a book, *Look Homeward Angel.*

That stuff about a window on time sounds like something Crowe would say.

Thomas Wolfe wrote a story called *The House of the Far and Lost* and I reckon that's where I've wandered down to, the house of the far and lost.

If feelin sorry for yourself paid anything you'd have a pocketful of money, he said.

She fell silent, thinking her thoughts. He silent as well, trying to divine them.

I know your're foolin with me, he finally said.

I'm not fooling with you.

That's all right. I don't mind. Just so you know I know it.

She came over and sat beside him, leaned over and kissed him gently on the lips. He could smell her hair, felt it brush his throat.

Don't think I don't know it, he said. His voice sounded strange to himself.

Sometimes they stayed till almost dawn, the folks at the Muledick were never earlyrisers. A thin wash of faint pink would break on the reef of the eastern world and what you could see of the world looked new and fresh and mintperfect like a dawn in a world where man had not been yet conceived.

Pale fingers rose toward the stars, drowning them in

light. He watched them go out one by one.

You ever wonder what it'd be like to be up there with them stars? he asked her once.

Oh Lord. No. I'm still stuck on trying to figure what it's like in this mess down here.

The poolroom smelled of stale beer and cigarette smoke. A dim neon glass. He could hear the soft click of pool-balls.

Nobody paid him any mind. He approached and awaited the barkeep's attention. When the barkeep finally noticed him. How old are you sonny? He asked.

I ain't here to buy nothin, Yates said. I'm lookin for a feller. You know TC Swain?

I know of him, the barkeep said. What do you want with him?

I just need to see him.

The man on the stool next to Yates turned to study him. Another one of Swain's woodsrats coming into the barn. What happened boy, your mama tell you TC was your Pa?

Yates didn't even look at him. Does he come in here much?

He's in and out, the barkeep said. You might catch him here. He kin of yours?

Not hardly, Yates said. He took after a friend of mine and I aim to get even.

Something in Yates's eyes made the barkeep look away.

He took dinner at his camp in the honeysuckle, eaten atop a tie pile in the shade. He'd bought canned Vienna sausages and little crackers sandwiched with peanut butter and a Nehi Orange. The highway crossed the railroad by the tieyard and as he ate he'd glance up occasionally to look when cars slowed for the railroad crossing. He glanced up sharply when one throttled down for the track and accelerated sharply with a fullthroated roar of gussied mufflers. He stopped chewing as a car slewed on the gravel and braked for the tracks. It was a highbacked black Ford with bootlegger springs. He washed the mouthful of crackers down with the orange drink and set the bottle down and scrambled off the tiepile. By the time he was on the highway the car was gone in a smoking haze of scorched rubber. He began to lope after the car. It rightangled at the first cross street and went on. All he could tell was the car had two people, the driver and a redheaded woman. When he reached the sidestreet, he turned too. The car had gone on, turned again, and even when it was lost to his sight, he slowed and plodded on anyway.

It was midafternoon before he found the car. It was parked outside of town in front of a two-story house. Beyond it lay fields where the western sun, mottled red, silhouetted black trees that appeared dimensionless against the red sky. The building had an upstairs porch cantilevered over a yard where patchy grass was dying, looking over a row of dusty scragglylooking catalpa trees.

He walked casually past the house, hands in his pockets. A door on the second floor opened and a woman came out onto the balcony. Yates hunched his shoulders and looked ahead down the street, but she paid him no

mind. She had on a black slip and her red hair was un-
done. She was drinking a bottle of beer. She leaned over
the balcony watching a rangy black cat forage a garbage
can beneath a catalpa tree. She drained the bottle and took
careful aim but when she hurled the bottle the cat was
gone like India ink flowing down the side of the can and
the bottle smashed on the lid.

Yates hurried on.

A pale moon had long risen, gleaming wistfully
through a reef of gauzy clouds and thus showed him the
way once he had passed the last streetlight. The concrete
and macadam ended and the dirt road began, a pale corridor of white dust leading away between borders of dark
blurred trees.

The houses had fallen away to unlighted shacks with
guarddogs chained to cartires with nothing much to guard
that Yates could see and they seemed to sense this for they
let him pass. In the last yard he came upon a ball and bat
and glove lying abandoned and he picked up the bat and
ball and went on idly swinging along the bat and tossing
the ball up and catching it. He turned back toward the last
of the houses and tossed the ball into the air and swung
the bat as hard as he could, leaning his entire weight into
it. There was a satisfying clean crack and the white sphere
went highballing invisibly into the night. He went on
down the white road swinging the bat.

The trees bordering the road were choked with
honeysuckle that seemed stronger in the dark or else his
senses heightened in the dark, for the odor of the honeysuckle was sweet and oppressive, an essence of all the
honeysuckles there were. He moved through a perpetual
silence, night birds falling silent at his approach then taking up the call behind him.

The house came up ghost white above the catalpa

tree, the roof gleaming darkly with dew. At the edge of the yard he hunkered in the shadow of a tree, studying the house. The Ford was parked by the ditch at the yard's edge, a door standing open, as if it had been abandoned to hasty flight. He waited a time and he couldn't hear anything at all and there was no sign of a light. He wondered what time it was. He judged it three o'clock or later and he did not expect to see anyone about. He got up and approached the car. He squatted at its four wheels, one after the other, using a twig against the valve core to flatten the tires, squatting in the fetid breath of air hissing out. He went carefully up the wrought iron stairway. It looked insubstantial and was appended to the walk in some manner he couldn't discern and he tried experimentally a time or two with his weight before venturing up it. Well, he thought, somebody's got to do it and I guess it's me.

At the top landing he stopped, rearing wildly back at his own reflection wrought on the dark glass. Behind him, the pale moon and the night gleamed over his shoulder like a bright familiar.

It'll be locked, Yates told himself, and switched hands holding the ballbat and lefthanded reached for the knob. It wasn't. It opened silently on oiled hinges and he stood nakedly exposed in the doorway peering into formless darkness. Gradually his eyes adjusted and by the waning moon, shapes began to attain solidity. A bed against the wall, tousled covers, two pale naked bodies like beached seaforms drowned by air. He eased into the room, each step painfully slow and absolutely silent.

He leant in the poor light peering at the sleeping bodies. A pale tangle of arms and legs, her arms and legs thrown out like someone lying crumbled, fallen from a great height. Red hair black as jet against her skin.

His eye had found immediately what he was looking

for, a dark pool of clothes at the side of the bed. So far
across the room, slow, creepmouse, creeping. The belt-
ed jeans were heavy and he didn't even wonder if there
was money in there, he could tell instantly there was. He
fished it out, feeling crumpled bills, greasy cold change.
He let it alone. There was a little blue Smith and Wes-
son revolver. He unhinged the cylinder and one by one
pushed the bullets out with a pen and pocketed them and
put the pistol back into Swain's pocket. A little insurance
never hurt nobody, he thought. He eyed the door with
the yard spread out below him white as milk, then he
hunkered for a moment clasping the ballbat before him
listening to the quiet breathing behind him. Well hell, he
said aloud.

He stood by the bed.

Swain, he said softly. He waited, holding the bat.

Swain, he said again.

Swain mumbled something incoherent. He smelled
like whiskey and old sweat.

Up and at em, Swain, Yates said. Rise and shine.

Swain rolled over onto his stomach. He pillowed
his head on the woman's chest. Be there in a minute, he
mumbled. I'm lookin for my shoes.

The ballbat cracked explosively, wood against flesh
and Swain screamed hoarsely and the bat came down
across his buttocks again and he sprang up still screaming
with the bat slamming against his shoulder and knocking
him sideway. He was holding his arms to protect his head
and trying to grab the bat, he was screaming whoo, whoo.
The girl rolled out of bed on the other side and fell over a
night table and staggered up drunkenly saying, What on
earth, what on earth.

Yates was flailing with the bat like a madman killing snakes. Glass broke, furniture was flying, Swain ad-

vanced on him then lurched backward when the tip of the bat glanced off his head. He got a hand on the bat. Yates jerked hard and recovered the bat but when he did, he fell and was sitting on the floor with Swain stumbling toward him. He swung the bat as hard as he could at Swain's legs. Something popped and went sideways like a gate on a broken hinge. Yates was already halfway to the door. Swain tried to rise but his leg folded under him and he fell with a hoarse cry.

Yates took the stairsteps two at a time and looking back, saw Swain's head and shoulders cross the threshold as if he were chasing him on hands and knees. Yates jumped the rest of the way to the ground. The pistol went click click click behind him. When he was in the yard he halted, breathing hard with hands on knees. He went on up the white road keeping close to the thick border of honeysuckle should he have to take to the timber. He never did and after awhile he threw the bat into woods.

One day from the rim of a cavernous openpit mine he watched a man climbing up a mountain of rock from the crusher. It looked like Swain. He wondered if Swain was vindictive enough to hunt him down and shoot him like a dog and he developed a fear of being taken in his sleep by Swain and he grew cagey as a hunted beast in his sleeping habits.

There was a graveyard far back on a ridge with crumbling rocks dating so far back the weather had worn them indecipherable and no one was buried here anymore and he took to sleeping there. He figured no one would bother him in a burying ground but one night he was brought instantly out of his drowsing by the sound of noises. He lay stiff and unmoving in fear, listening to a vague sourceless muttering of the dead he couldn't make out the words to.

The voices grew louder and he could hear footfalls shuffling along the dirt logroad. He leapt up and looked all about. He was hit by a wave of relief so strong it left him giddy.

A drunk black man was shuffling along the road toward home, coming back from the dance at the schoolhouse, talking loudly and gesturing and carrying two sides of the conversation.

I told that bitch, I said, bitch, he was saying when Yates hailed him from his seat on a gravestone. Yates lifted an arm. Hidy, he called.

The drunk halted, instantly peering toward the graveyard rearing back wildly, eyes rolling whitely and his hands thrown up protectively against the bared and lonesome specter before him, giving a whinny of absolute fear and fleeing the way he'd come, at some point forsaking the road, for Yates could hear him thrashing through the bracken.

A few days later Yates was in Dow Cook's store and he learned from the old men he was a familiar of that the old graveyard back on the ridge had been proven once and for all to be haunted, and it was a good place to avoid.

First day on my own and a goddamned cat ate my dinner, Yates said. Had me one of them fried pies. Cat eat it. Eat my bread. Lucky I had me a can of wieners and the cat didn't know how to run a can opener. If it had, I'd been fucked.

Where you stayin now? Crowe asked him.

Whippoorwill City I call it. Them sons of a bitch hollerin at one another all night long and drive me crazy. A man can't even think straight. What do you reckon they're sayin?

I wouldn't know, Crowe said. I never learned the language.

Yates stirred sugar into his coffee, watched the granules swirl and dissolve in the hot liquid. He cupped his hand about the mug as if he drew comfort from the warmth.

I got to find me some place out of the wind.

You're welcome to stay here. All I got is one cot but we can take turns about sleeping on the floor. I got a stove, too. I reckon you couldn't lower yourself to live with a nigger, Crowe said.

That don't enter into it. The truth is I don't like trouble and this is the best way out of it. I busted his damn leg with a bat and he'll be lookin for me. Hell, he emptied a pistol at me. You had words with him before and I ain't causin no more trouble between you and him.

When there's trouble between me and him he'll cause it, not you.

Whoever then. Anyway, there's been enough of it. I've about got used to doin without walls anyhow. Seems like they smother me. I can't breathe right.

Crowe studied this apprentice wildman, fugitive of walls and mothers and drunks. Who'd grown to unaccustomed long silence and whose eyes held a strangely distant look.

Sooner or later you'll have to go back, Crowe said. A

man always goes back home. I had a home and a mother I might go myself. Crowe was silent a time. He began to roll a cigarette. I may kill the son of a bitch just for the hell of it, he said. A good killin would fix him right up.

He went out in a foggy misty predawn light with biscuits and meat in a floursack knotted at the top. When he passed the gap in the fence roosters were proclaiming the day and mist rolled out of the hollow behind the barn like smoke. He didn't look back until he topped out on the ridge and when he did, all Allen's Creek looked smoky from cookfires and somewhere he could smell the bright nostalgic odor of cedar burning. A line of fire crept the eastern rim of the world. He turned his face toward it and went on.

He couldn't bring himself to return to his mother and was unwilling to inconvenience Crowe. He had been out over a week when he found the cave and even when he found it, it was by accident and he didn't know it for what it was. It did not look like a cave. It just looked like a hole in the ground. The opening was triangulated by three flat tables of limestone and was roughly three feet across the base and five feet in length. It was almost hidden by the coppery branches of an enormous cedar the wind had blown down.

He peered down eight feet or so below where he could see the floor by the noonday sun. Shit a brick, he said to himself. The nearwhite limestone looked as flat as a living room floor. He couldn't see any walls though walls there must be and he had to figure a way in and out.

He had seen immediately that he was not the first person here. Two or three feet down the ruins of a home-cobbled ladder leant its top against a rock shelf with its feet resting on the limestone floor. The ladder was made of two trimmed hickory saplings with rungs tied across with leather thongs. It had a distinctly old look about it but he figured he had to test it.

He had to hang onto the limestone with his arms and he was chestdeep into the hole feeling about with his feet when his toes touched the top rung. With the first tentative application of pressure the dryrotted wood gave and the thongs crumbled and he hauled himself back up and squatted peering into the hole. Dryrotted wood drifted down in a white powdery dust and settled delicately on the floor he had already begun to think of as his own.

He was back in thirty minutes with part of a treetop with limbs broken off in makeshift rungs that he figured would serve as a temporary stairway and he lowered it carefully buttfirst into the hole and when he had it positioned to his satisfaction he squirreled down it.

When he was on the floor he looked quickly about. The shitfire, he said. The room was sixteen or eighteen feet in diameter and was crudely rectangular. He thought at first it was some sort of exploratory ore shaft but it was too crude and natural looking for that and the room itself had not been quarried from stone but was some sort of natural formation. Walls of solid limestone, the northern side sat slightly aslant and the south one as well, so that the room was shaped roughly the shape of Tennessee on a road map. The ceiling sloped and was bulbous with slabs of rock that looked as if they'd been caught in another rock and seized there when it cooled, but the floor was relatively flat and no rougher than finished concrete.

Where the ceiling sloped in one corner the floor rose

to meet it and there was an opening two or three feet in diameter he figured to explore later. He wouldn't have been surprised at anything, a hall leading to a bathroom with trollsize appointments, a kitchen with hammered copper utensils and little appliances of stone.

A man could throw a square dance in here, he said aloud. His voice sounded strange, amplified, imbued with authority, and he said it again, A man could throw a square dance in here.

He hunkered against the wall and just studied the place, with an eye perhaps toward furniture placement had he furniture to place. The ceiling was blackened in places by old fires and a burntlooking place as well on the stone floor, but it was so ancient and timescoured it was no longer black but sooty gray and his mind dwelt for a time on who had built them. What they were like. Their voices had amplified strangely as his had, had echoed hollowly stone to stone. What had they said? What tongue had they spoken? Maybe Indians, he thought, holding counsel here, leaving for the hunt or on mounted warparties. He didn't know what come before Indians, but he guessed it could have been them. He grew momentarily dizzy from thinking about such leaps of time and he thought whatever game had been spitted over these fires might not even exist anymore, some strange feral beast whose appearance was beyond his ability to reckon.

Here in the cave, the weary telluric dark past and present intersected seamlessly and he saw how there was no true beginning or end and that all things once done were done forever and went spiraling outward fainter and fainter like ripples on water and that the face of a young girl carried at once within her a bitter harridan and past that the satinpillowed deathbed of the grave.

He shook off these thoughts and climbed back up his

ladder. He was already thinking about some sort of rope ladder he could either remove and replace or conceal and he figured to lay in a supply of wood. The woods were full of dry windfalls for the taking and he'd lug sections of them to the hole and roll them in until they mounded halfway to the door then after a time he went back down the ladder and arranged it in an enormous stack against one wall. He went back up his ladder with a sense of well-being. Shitfire, he said. All I need is window curtains and a mailbox and I'm set.

He bought a can of cornbeef hash and two nickel cakes at Dow Cook's store. He bought a dope and ordered up crackers which Dow took out of a barrel and wrapped up neatly in white butcher's paper.

Crackers too, Dow marveled. I may go to the house early today after such an order as this. It ain't ever day I sell a bill of groceries like this one.

Yates didn't even reply. Dow didn't like him and he made no effort to pretend otherwise. He hadn't liked him since the episode with the pocketknife and he felt he was still owed money but he never said so. There had been a moment when he'd inadvertently looked deep into Crowe's eyes and he hadn't in the least liked what he'd seen there. He'd felt himself throatcut, already, dead and buried, faint singing in the backyard. But he didn't see that in Yates's eyes and he wasn't afraid of him.

I need me a poke, Yates said. I got a long way to tote this stuff.

I don't doubt it a bit, Dow said, handing across the

brown paper bag. Nor any idea where you'll be when you git there.

He went out with the screendoor slamming behind him on its too tight keeperspring and went around the building. Dow lived behind the storebuilding on a little rise with his chickenhouse set near the branchrun. Yates glanced about. The only person he could see was old Mrs. Cook chopping corn in newground far up the hollow behind the house and her bonneted head seemed turned away and he doubted she could have seen him anyway. He went swiftly up the branchrun stone to stone through a heady altar of hedge roses and into the fetid shade of the chicken house. He did not window shop. He went rapidly nest to nest bagging half a dozen or so eggs and was into the hedge roses again even before the chickens began cackling. He paused halfway up the hillside and through a break in the wall of greenery saw the back door of the store open. Dow Cook came out and just stood looking appraisingly at the henhouse. Then he went back in.

He boiled two of the eggs and put the rest away with one of the cakes in a little shelf in the wall he figured to use for a larder. When the eggs were done he peeled and ate them slowly between bites of the hash watching the fire flicker and the smoke rise in a slow stately circular motion.

He was picking his teeth and wishing he'd thought to acquire some coffee somewhere and perhaps a little salt when he noticed bemusedly that none of the smoke seemed to go into the stone hallway. The opening in the roof acted as a natural flue drawing off the smoke and in some curious way there seemed to be something pushing it from the opening of the corridor.

He went in on his hands and knees. It was cold in here, a summer home perhaps, you'd not want to winter here. What light there was tended rapidly away to nothingness after a few feet and he began to strike matches. He was in a sort of shaft running downward through the earth. It widened and heightened past the entrance but still its height was such that he could not stand fully erect. He went crouching cautiously into the darkness, a darkness blacker when the matches died. With the ghosts of the matches flaring inside his eyelids and his hands outstretched before him like a blind man feeling his way.

He could feel cold air faint on his face. Not exactly a breeze but not exactly like anything else either. He halted and lit his next to last match. He seemed to be at the end of a stone corridor, rocks scattered about, slabs of rock tilted against the wall like mummy cases. The corridor ended abruptly in an abutment of solid stone and he couldn't fathom where the cold air was coming from. He began to feel around the walls. He felt the air stronger around the edge of an upright rock. He struck a match and held it toward the rock and when he did it immediately flared and died. He tried to push the rock aside but it wouldn't push. He pressed his feet and he pushed until lights began to flicker in his head and his legs trembled and he sat down to think about it awhile.

He guessed he might could move it with a pinch bar but he didn't have a pinch bar. He didn't have any more matches either.

What I need is me a goddamned hardware store, he said aloud.

He began to crawl back toward the light.

I need me a box of matches, he told Dow Cook.

Be a penny, Dow said, sliding them across the counter. Twice in one day. I'm glad I stayed open awhile longer. I may take to opening of a Sunday just in case the notion strikes you to come in and buy a little somethin.

Yates pocketed the matches. One of these days I'm goin to come in here with a thousand dollars and look around awhile for things to spend it on. Then I'm goin to go spend it somewheres else.

Any thousand dollars you ever have would have to have the ink blowed dry on it, Dow said, and I wouldn't want no part of it.

The pinch bar was no problem either. In a mining settlement there seems to be pieces of scrap steel every-where and Yates could pick and choose. He found a four-foot rod an inch and a half or so thick, leant against one of the furnace flues. It had one end heated and beaten flat so that it was just what he was looking for and seemed to have been made solely for the purpose of Yates moving a large rock with it. He looked up. Hawks wheeled about the dizzy precipice and he wondered what the world might look like from there.

He shouldered it and struck out once again for the ridge.

Behind the post office, among old uncoppered barrel stoves and a motley of garbage strewn among five-gallon buckets, he found one half full of stiff vis-cous tar and paddles that had been used for patching the roof and an armful of tarstained rags. He smeared the paddles with tar and wrapped rags lightly around them. He kept on, alternating layers of rags and tar, until he had a pile of flares he felt anybody would have been proud of.

After a time he caught the hang of it, taking just enough bite for the tip of the bar to catch and leaning such weight as he had into his work to move the rock aside a fraction of an inch at a time. He could feel the cold air, like breath blowing out of a tomb, stronger all the time, and after a while the pinch bar didn't work anymore. He guessed he'd moved the edge of the rock past the opening and there was nothing for the bar to get purchase on. It finally occurred to him to try below or above the opening and alternating low and high. He continued to winch the rock aside until the opening seemed wide enough for him to squeeze through.

To where he didn't know. He leaned the bar carefully against the wall and he took up one of the torches and lit it. The tar flame flared and guttered into darting blue points of flame then caught in earnest, flaming backward in the draft. There were two or three feet of stone that seemed to just stop and beyond that there was only darkness. A darkness the like of which he'd never seen. Light seemed scarcely to defray it. Not just a negation of light, but a tangible substance with weight and mass. All he could see through the hole when he pushed the torch through was a sleek black floor sloping away and it seemed to end where the light ended. Drops of melted tar dripped in little blue spurts like a rain of fire and died on the wet black rock. He scrambled through the hole and lit another torch and, with the first, raised them aloft.

Oh, sweet Jesus, he said, without meaning to or even knowing what it was he said and fell into a wonderstruck silence.

He had come to a world within a world. Light fanned out from him into the darkness where the light vanished before there was anything to see. All there was was the slick black obsidian he stood on and the rock behind him. There seemed nothing above him save a dark anti-sky, profoundly starless. Nothing before him save blackness that seemed absolutely unreckonable, a limitless enormity or the smallest thing there ever was. He'd taken one misstep and found himself on barren rocks in the starless depths of interstellar space.

He looked back once as if to get a fix on the door behind him, like something talismanic to ward off whatever beasts dwelt here and crouched to offset the steepening slope as he went down the rock with the fire wavering back. He suddenly noticed how profound the silence was. He halted with an involuntary expulsion of breath at the edge of an inkblack sea that stretched away out of sight, flat and motionless as a mirror of ebony. Nothing moved. There was nothing to move. He turned. Shapes like vague prehistoric monolithic rocks in a silver drifting mist formed themselves like images in a dream.

Suddenly one torch guttered and died, and the dark seemed to leap at him, a tangible wall of breathless oppression he could feel constricting his lungs and he was assailed by such fear as he'd never known. He whirled to locate his exit and just as he did the remaining torch went out and dark fell sudden as a thunderclap and he went scrabbling like an animal, like some kind of alien and lowly seaform scuttling up the slick rock toward his den. When he reached it, he went through it panicstricken and breathing raggedly not feeling his shirt tear or the sharp rocks cut into his flesh.

He watched a triangle of stars. He'd made his bed beneath the opening in the ceiling for the view it afforded, and the stars swam and drifted in the smoke. He'd a fire that gave the chamber a hellish orange glow that flickered and warped the walls and from time to time this small troglodyte would rise from his bed of rags and tend it. There didn't seem to be enough light to suit him and he kept throwing on more wood.

Lying so and watching a rind of pale moon track into his vision he thought of what had struck deepest about the world he'd seen: it seemed absolutely new, unused, unmarked. There were no scratches in the rock, no animal droppings or teethscored bones, no pottery shard or bits of chipped flint. Little by little he came to accept a truth he did not want to accept, that his were the first human eyes to lay sight on this dark netherworld. All the millions of years had come and gone and mutated and adapted and whole species had ceased to exist and countless eons of folks' lives had clacked away unnoticed while the still black waters lay and the wet obsidian gleamed, waiting for light to reflect before fire even existed and waiting for the chink of his pinch bar on the stone.

It was a long time before he slept and when he did it was troubled sleep like a feverdream and he dreamed of blind sleek forms that knifed the bottomless waters of an inkblack lake.

Slow grievous days followed then, with the rains beginning. These days seemed unending and every day it rained, a gray and spiritless creeping rain out of a gunmetal sky. Slow season of dying, the world seemed to be in mourning for some obscure loss. Daylong he'd sit about his den waiting for a shift in the weather, his life to change, anything. A deep somber gloom crept into the grotto that housed him. He'd go out but there seemed nothing to do, nowhere to go, no one worth talking to. The ceaseless rain fell and the trees dripped until it seemed to seep into his very soul. His life had eddied into the backwaters, the sluggish sloughs where nothing moved, and for the first time he felt volitionless, unfocused, stalemated.

Looking up from his armful of gathered wood that wasn't waterlogged he searched the sky for geese fleeing south. He couldn't see them but he could hear their high lonesome cries and something lost in their voices bespoke change, ill weather, hard times, as if they were taking all there was of life worth keeping with them and leaving only a barren world of skeletal trees and rainwet stone and winds that already whispered the implicit threat of ice.

By night he'd tend his wavering fire and glance uneasily at the rim of dripping darkness as if he was waiting for something. Standing some obscure and purposeful watch, he began to feel himself accompanied by ghosts of his own past and voices he'd forgotten or paid no heed to returned to haunt him. These voices conversed dreadfully, familiar timbres, cadences, held discourse among themselves of which he could make out no word. Water strung off the rim of rock and formed a pool on the grotto floor then a stream in the channel of rock and ran off toward the tunnel, and deep in the night he could hear water running.

A great black cat prowled wraithlike through his dreams. It was an enormous black panther of languorous grace whose territory was marked not by woods or hills or mountains but by the perimeters of the very world itself, who came and went at his whim and asked no man's say-so. Imbued with a languid supple coilspring tension that hinted at its casual deadliness, its eyes lanternyellow and sinister, as depthless and unreadable as glass.

The cat prowled the cave at will as it might its own lair nor did it acknowledge even the limits of dreams for he came struggling and crying awake one night with its dark face looking down into his own as if it might steal his breath as such cats were told to do and the yellow eyes bore into his own and seemed to glow from some force internal and exist independent of any light they might reflect. Somehow he knew it bode him no ill will and was there to show him something but he was frozen, he couldn't move, he was holding his breath. The cat turned soundless and padded across the cave floor. It paused beneath the triangle of rain and crouched and leapt to the rim with a contemptuous ease and merged with the night and was gone.

He came down the long spine of the ridge sometime past midnight in the darkness, his feet finding the way by habit and by the worn repletion of the years, the stars dishing and jauncing with his rapid steps on the stone and owls crying at his back as if he trespassed here in some void no longer his domain.

He came down the hollow past his childhood playhouse and past his abandoned fish box where perhaps even now the ghosts of pale sleek shapes moved in its mossy covered bottom. From the ridge there'd been a moment when he'd thought her lamp alight but he saw now it had been a trick of the starlight, for the house was still as a forgotten graveyard. The windows seemed paned with smooth squares marvelously crafted from the dark itself.

He'd eased cautiously around the corner, cautiously onto the porch, wary eyes glancing all about. As if he'd meet someone coming out as he went in. Swain, other men he didn't know, or want to know, his childhood self. There was no one. The house might have been abandoned, given up to weeds and the delicate forays of mice and nearsilent padding of predators. An old shoe lay curled in the shadow of the ivy like the dried and ossified remains of some experimental lifeforms that had not worked out.

The wall lay white in the moonlight with the inkblack etchings of ivy shadows, intricate as lace filigree. This door, like all doors, a door you can open and enter into or a world you can turn away from and leave unknown. His shadow loomed on it.

He twisted the knob and pushed the door, and the unplumb door when he released it slapped softly against the wall. He stepped into the room speaking her name into a silence his voice didn't break, and he went on feeling his way into the darkness that should have been familiar to him but had some undercurrent of the strange.

From the moment he stepped into the room he'd been subconsciously aware of the smell, a sweet subtle smell of the beginning of decay, there was a hum of wings as if insects perpetually droned here. He was feeling for the lamp. He unglobed it and struck a match on his beltbuckle. There was an odor of coal oil and when he globed the lamp the room sprang into harsh yellow relief.

She was sitting in the rocking chair staring at him. Coalblack blood had dried all down her front and a hardened puddle in her lap where her hands cupped like claws. She was leaning sideways in the chair stiffened by rigor mortis and crawling with flies and when he steeled himself and approached her and touched her shoulder lightly she tilted away and fell and he clasped his eyes as if he'd claw them from his head and screamed such a cry of outrage and bereavement and utter revulsion as should have sent the fabric of night to whatever light lay beyond and stitched a momentary caesura in the clockwork of the world itself and then he fled blindly back into the night.

I'm an orphan, Yates cried.

He willed himself to make his body immutable as stone and imperishable to the harshest weathers that the world could send. He stared across the grave and across the preacher whose worn hands kept trying to stay the windrustled pages and to shield them from the first slant drops of rain the wind brought. Across the valley to the far soft-folded hills the hollows lay in dark secrecy and where pale mist rose, doves called mournfully as hawks rode the updrafts of winds like vaguely chastening kites of metallic feathers.

They were watching. He tried very hard to think of nothing at all. Then as if some wall inside him gave, with a grinding of breached brick and mortar, he suddenly saw her face with a clarity that seemed scoured with acid. She was in the coffin with one red rose clasped in her lifeless gray hand and death had somehow imbued her face with a primness it had never possessed in life, a look that somehow reminded him of a school teacher. There was a cast of betrayal about her mouth as if he ought to have not let the thing happen and her face in waxen effigy looked profoundly beyond any kindness he might do for her or any cruelty. Without knowing he was going to, he twisted away and she made no move to stop his flight.

In the last windblown days of Indian summer he had nowhere to be nor any soul in all the world to answer to. Daylong he might sit on the slope above the house where he once had lived and watch the pale undersides of the silver maple leaves run like quicksilver in the windy light and he had a thought for the encumbrances of freedom and for the childhood he'd willingly cast aside and could not retrieve. Already the wind held a steely hint of winter and above the windy sedge the sky was a clear blue with a look of unreckonable distances.

He lay with his hands laced behind his head and he studied the minutiae of the days and the subtle shadings of light and shift of shadows as the sun refracted in orange fire from the windowpanes. In images that seemed etched into his mind behind these windowpanes, she padded silently about the kitchen in mindless ritual as again and again she tilted away from the weight of his hand in her attendant welter of greenflies, and the finality of these things appalled him a little: could he have altered these absolutes one iota with the flesh and blood and bones that were all he owned out of the vast world's riches, he would have done so, but he could not. He'd not known the world was so filled with things for which there were no second chances.

She lay far back on a ridge among others of her kind. Among those dead from disease or from misadventures, dead from childbirth gone awry or those Saturday night throatcuts, part of the vast harvest from the vagaries of life. Unmarked in life, and so in death, the grave distinguished only by the oval of raw earth beneath the cedars. Beyond the blind eyes of the sleeping dead the world fell breathlessly, faded away in countless horizons, the last one fading to a soft transparency.

Ill kept and graceless he came out of the blue dusk like a wraith. Thin and intense in clothes too big for him that seemed tailored by the weathers or the rough country he'd become a familiar of.

He'd drift among the graves like a prospective customer of whatever dread wares were up for sale here and in the blowing leaves and failing light, the only thing that separated him from these still and cold folk seemed a few feet of loamy earth. He'd come to suspect madness worried his tracks like a homeless dog he could not get shut of. He'd glimpse it out of the corner of his eye, a lean black slatribbed hound with a long brown muzzle but then he'd turn and there'd be nothing.

His mind was a dark torrent of thoughts, but he could not articulate them and could he have transformed them to words there were no ears to hear them. He'd hunker beneath the cedar there with the trunk of the cedar against his back and the soft rush of the branches above him and he did not even suspect why he was here.

Fall ended abruptly and the early winter brought a hard freeze that seized everything in ice. Each blossom, each twig, each zygotic leaf. The muddy earth erupted in crystal spumes of ice and he hugged himself against a bitter wind that had shifted northward. Beneath the wavering bowl of orange light his bonfire formed and peering upward into the frozen heavens Yates could see the very air freezing before his eyes. Glittering crystals of frost formed and drifted weightlessly earthward and vanished in the fire and beyond the wall of heat a circle of hoarfrost formed on the earth around him. He suspected some suspension of the natural laws, some aberration, somebody asleep at the wheel. Senility or madness had overtaken whatever god controlled the weathers. The next night a slow mournful rain fell and it grew cold and the ceaseless rain dampened until he could feel it even beneath the outcropping of rock he crouched under and it was a long time before he slept.

He woke after midnight shivering and thought of fire but he had no kindling. Piss on this, he said after a time. He got up sore and stiff from the stone he'd pillowed himself on and went down the hillside and crossed a stream shrouded with spectrelike gouts of pale foam that had come out of its banks. He came out in a fallow field where groundfog lay white and opaque as snow, cows stood in solitary lumps of solidity in the ephemeral rain and up again through a border of thornroses onto the baked hardpan of the road. He could hear the river now. The company store slept unlit, locked and darkened by the rain. He went on toward Gander Ridge and up it toward what had once been his home, a dark bulk against the deeper dark of the cedars.

He crouched watching his house from the shelter of a windfall pine. He watched the place afraid to approach it. Who knew where Swain might turn up, he was rootless as smoke and might be anywhere. Swain himself might be hunkered in a darkened corner cradling an axe like some beast of childhood nightmare. Yet there was no smoke from the chimney, no lights. He thought about his mother. He had a thought for the chill of the night, for wayfarers on the road, for the cold hard bluffs where he'd pillow his head.

The known world telescoped inward on itself. A chill wind carried a few tentative flakes of snow, leaves clashed softly like faint distant chimes. He'd been living out in the open until he felt barely human. Just something resembling other folk yet with some grim twist to mark it, set out in these hills and brush arbors like some outlandish mascot to the human race, some cautionary reminder of what can happen when your luck goes south. It was turning colder yet and last night he'd dreamed of the living room stove and his bed.

Goddamn, he said aloud. Somebody might as well be getting the use of it.

He took up the club he'd taken to carrying and wound down the hillside toward the house. With its rusted roof and weathered dark planking the house seemed a focus for drawing off such light as there was, each waning day sucked through failing windowpanes to the dark beneath the beds, the sooty corners of the closets.

He entered and thumbbolted the door behind him with some caution but there was only the smell of dead ashes, cold still air, a sort of humming silence. The first thing he looked for was the lamp and he lit it and reglobed it and stood for a moment clasping the globe bothhanded for the yellow kerosene heat. Then he turned his attention to the heating stove. It was packed almost full with wadded newspapers and grocery bags and he found some more and jammed them in along with a dress that wasn't needed by anyone and an ancient straw hat that had a combustible look about it.

Then he paused and looked about the room. There was nothing around save the silence. Nothing but a wall calendar from some lost year where a trio of angels simpered in defiance of gravity from a hillock of clouds. He thought of his mother and her own cindered wings and

despair hung in the corners of the room like smoke. He
knelt and lit the newspapers and wandered into the kitch-
en in the off chance that she might have left any food.
He hadn't had a warm meal in he didn't know how many
days and he envisioned a hot meal and an hour or two
basking before the fire. Then maybe he'd bar the door and
hope Swain was somewhere else for the night and take a
chance on sleeping in his bed.

He found an unlabeled can which when opened
proved to be corned beef hash and he raked it into a saucepan and carried it into the living room and set it atop the
heater. Then he noticed the fire had gone out.

Why won't you burn, you cold son of a bitch, he
asked it.

He found the kerosene can and shook it to gauge its
contents and upended it and hurled a cup of kerosene over
the papers and when he dropped a match in this time it
met his expectations. There was a thump when the coaloil
caught and an immediate scrabbling inside the heater as
if the very fire itself was made animate, intent on scrambling free of the confines and a moment of panicked primeval fear touched him.

Well, what the hell, he thought.

The papers exploded in billowing orange flames and
he was buffeted by an enormous wave of heat. He could
hear the fire sucking up the chimney like a freight train.

That's more by God like it, he said.

He was sitting crouched before the fire eating corned
beef hash with a spoon when he heard a strange sound. He
cocked his head sideways, listening. He'd had his ears at-
tuned for Swain's car or his step on the porch but this was
a different sort of sound: a sort of hissing keening that rose
to a hoarse croaking screech. He kept looking about the
room but the sound seemed sourceless, something out of

the very ether. Yates was a believer in signs and portents, and he wondered was this a warning of something dire. He threw open the front door of the stove and peered in momentarily and glimpsed some dark form imbued with urgency capering in the flames, then an enormous flaming rat erupted from the depths of the stove in a welter of burning paper like a salamander scattering the firecoals of hell. It was garneteyed in the flames and, with paws outstretched like a flying squirrel riding the cusp of an explosion it leapt upon him. Arhh, Yates cried. Wideeyed and fallen backwards he was trampled as the rat shot over him and went scrambling across the floor. Its hot little footprints, the smell of burning oil and hair. On the braided rug it left little seedlets of fire like vermin spreading a flaming plague. It fetched up against a wall and spun and came at him again like some demented windup toy. The enormous rat cavorted and danced in a wild frenzy, reeking with smoke and kerosene, flaming blindly in a slipstream of sparks, flames and fire and slamming into walls and climbing the curtains and leaping among the bedclothes. Everything it touched fell under the plague of the fire.

You're strowin it everwhere, Yates cried.

He'd come up with the broom and like the participant in some bizarre game was batting at the furiously animate rat. It had climbed the window curtains and he knocked it free but behind it left small hot flames like roses. He was batting at the rat with the broom where it wheeled unmindful of him and he could see its tiny agate eyes with unfocused malevolence as it shot past him. He knocked the curtains down and began to try to beat out the flames but the wallpaper was crept by an erotic pattern of fire and behind him the bed was a pillar of flames. The room was filling up with hot yellow smoke that bellied against the ceiling. The paper the room was ceilinged with began to curl and smolder.

He looked wildly about. He ran into the kitchen for the water bucket but there was no water and he hurled the empty pail into the rising tide of fire. The rat lay still and smoking in a corner of the room. Yates began hopping about the room stamping out little patches of fire but others erupted as burning paper unreeled and dropped from the ceiling. At last he took up the saucepan and the spoon and went out.

It burned all night. He kept restoking it with the charred buttends of rafters and floor joists. It was a long night. Daylight found him crouched at the outer perimeter of an almost perfect circle of ash, his hands outstretched for what heat there was, and he seemed only vaguely human. Something that once had been or held minimal promise of becoming. The rain still softly fell and the wind had laid so that he could hear it hissing softly in the hot ashes. There was no look at all on his face, as if he'd been bereft of all thought at once by a sudden glimpse at the decrepit shifting scaffolding the world was supported by, his eyes seared by that blinding glimpse into the machinations of the world itself as if he was overcome by profound weariness. All his senses seemed to have shut down as if they'd suffered some sort of overload. Above this charred ruin wan smoke drifted listlessly and the soft rain hissed in the hot ashes. He knew he should be on the move, but he didn't know where to and he was loath to leave the fire. It was the first time he'd been warm in days.

When the Pastor Meecham came he came alone, and out of some personal idiosyncrasy he went to the one place he must have known Yates wouldn't be. Sure enough, Yates wasn't taking the air where his porch used to be and the preacher, at his leisure, studied the charred ruin with a bemused speculation. The trees that had shrouded the house were burned too, just the charred twisted bones of trees, and he guessed they'd burned like torches in the night. He wished he could have seen it.

First the woman and then this. Not just the woman strangling to death by the revolt of her own life's blood but the very den where she'd practiced her whoring in and who knew what else and the very bed she'd done it in rendered to ash. Not content with the woman, he had sent his terrible messenger of fire and burned the infestation to the ground. Watching all this from the wagonseat his face wore a look almost beatific, as if he'd wrought this ruin himself or seen his own prophecy come to fruition.

If he climbed down and kicked through the ashes he had no doubt he could have unearthed the charred leathery bodies of demons. Their little batlike faces, their needlesharp teeth, claws forever sheathed. They'd infested the walls, crept the joists and rafters, capered behind the weatherboarding like rats.

They had been hearing the wagon for some time and the boy was studying the ridge when it appeared. Yates's eyes, shaded with his hand, watched with something akin to apprehension as the mules' heads showed and with dread inevitability the team and wagon simultaneously froze black and stark against the cobalt sky for a moment, locked in an illusion of dimensionless motion like something possessing no reality of its own but simply symbolic of direr events yet to be. Then the wagon lurched down the hillside and the illusion of black depthlessness faded and it was simply a team of mules drawing a wagon with Meecham, erect, riding the brake. Yates looked away and spat.

There the son of a bitch comes, he said.

Crowe set his coffeecup carefully by his booted foot. He looked. He's dutybound all right, he said.

I left word everywhere for him. The post office, at Dow Cook's store. I even told em at the Muledick I ain't got nothing to say to him nor him to me. You see what good it done. Here the son of a bitch comes.

Crowe shook his head in amused commiseration. A man set on savin your soul ain't goin to let a little thing like what you want stand in his way, he said.

The wagon rolled on toward the house with Meecham slapping the lines and hurrying the mules down the road that was not a road as such but simply a winding grassless depression worn into the earth by years of wagonwheels following the same ruts. By the time it rolled into the yard and halted, Meecham's eye had already fixed on Yates ensconced comfortably on the porch, and the moment it did his face took on a vexed putupon cast. He paused for a moment as if awaiting invitation to alight and when none came climbed down anyway. He stood beside the wagon studying these curious malingerers. Then he strode on toward the house.

Boy you a hard feller to find, he said.

I ain't been lost that I know of, Yates said.

I ain't got much time on my hands, Meecham said abruptly. I can't sit on the porch daylong like some folks and watch the grass grow. I got a congregation to tend and sick folk to see to and I can't spend all my time runnin some halfgrown boy that ain't got the grace about him to be thankful for other folks' kindness.

I never set out to be no trouble, Yates said. But then again I never sent for you either.

No, you never, Meecham said. He hunkered in the bare yard and took up a stick and abstractedly began to draw meaningless hieroglyphs in the dirt. Nevertheless, you're a concern to certain members of my congregation. You a orphan now.

I can take care of myself, Yates said. I been on my own awhile.

I don't doubt you have, Meecham nodded. Still you had a mama then and you was her responsibility whether she stood up to it or not. Now other folks got that responsibility and they determined not to shirk it.

Hellfire, Yates said in frustration.

Meecham nodded. He was studying the meaningless henscratches he'd made in the clay as if they held the solution to all life's mysteries and he was committing them to memory. I expect you do have more than a nodding acquaintance with hellfire and in time to come you'll be even more familiar with it. God Almighty can turn hellfire to his own purpose. A little touch of it burned you out lock stock and barrel didn't it?

Shit a brick, Yates exploded. A rat burnt me out. A goddamned gopher the size of a housecat set the place on fire and went toward Paiton Holler just a shittin and gettin. I figured it burnt out everthing on Allen's Creek. I expect it was in all the papers.

Meecham absentmindedly fingered the fistsize purple black goiter on his neck. A malignancy already ticking like a timebomb, low and faint, he didn't even hear it yet. Yates watched him. His pale fanatic's eyes locked on to Jesus and tracking the lineaments of his face already taking on the cast of a finer world than this one.

I'll look over that blaspheming, Meecham said. You was brought up hard ways and hard ways is all you've knowed. It didn't burn everbody else though, did it? Just you. That ought to tell you something.

It tells me God Almighty wasn't even in the county, Yates said. I know a rat when I see one. Hellfire. It had a tail long as my arm. He looked at Crowe who had leant his head against a porch stanchion with his eyes closed. The corners of his mouth were downturned in a look of sardonic amusement.

I don't mind him sendin it, Yates said. He's callin the shots and he can send what he wants to. But if he'd a sent the son of a bitch somewheres besides my heatin stove I'd still have a roof over my head.

Brought up slipshod, he was used to making do with whatever fell to hand. The widow's farm seemed adorned with detail he couldn't help but judge as frivolous. Nonetheless these things were a wonder to him. There were martin boxes made from longnecked gourds painted and affixed atop poles and there was a gaudy duck whittled from wood and lacquered in garish colors like a cartoon duck whose wings turned in the wind and showed you which way the wind was blowing from. Gusts found him pointed into the wind, windmilling his whittled wings madly and grinning his foolish pointed beak into the elements.

He fell quickly into the way of things. There were tasks that had to be done and he was expected to do them. There were cows to be fed twice daily and a long poultry house where chicks were raised into marketable fryers. Long feeders that had to be kept full of cracked grain and waterers to fill and kerosene heaters that burned to keep them warm.

He liked the chicken house. It was always warm and comfortable, and it was kept as clean as possible with fresh sawmill shavings and it always smelled of wood and the faint ammonia smell of the chickens. The chickens seemed satisfied as long as there was food to eat and water to drink and folks hotfooting to their every need, though sudden noises were apt to drive them into a panic and they'd pile up into an enormous feathered ball and smother themselves to death if you didn't unpile them. He thought them without a doubt the stupidest creatures he'd ever had any dealings with.

He thought of them mainly as money. There was an enormous number of them and translated into coins of the realm he'd have been a man of means. Leant against the windows with the afternoon sun pale and slant on the moted glass, he'd dream about what to do if all this were his. Circumstances with a lawyer reading the will, and to my adopted son I bequeath all my worldly chickens. On further consideration this seemed too far down the line. She seemed far too young to be thinking of wills and dying. Perhaps she'd marry him, share and share alike. This was not beyond the realm of possibility. He saw himself at Dow's. A long black car parked in the shadows, Dow Cook obsequious, dragging out a ticket book two inches thick.

Put that down for you, Mr. Yates?

I reckon I'll just pay now, he'd say, pulling out a rubber banded roll of bills, carelessly peeling off a twenty.

Dusk fell early these first winter days and when he came in from the evening feeding, she'd be in the kitchen getting supper ready.

Them chickens got it better than people, he said, closing the door. Beyond him dusk was already settling, the trees still and coldlooking. The hollow already drowned in silent twilight.

She turned from the stove. What?

There's folks on Allen's Creek freezin to death all the winter. No groceries. Them chickens got people to tote em feed and water ever minute and heaters to keep em warm. A man'd be better off to be a chicken.

Well, you may be right. She was setting bowls on the table. Beans, potatoes, a platter of country ham. If your idea of better off is being plucked naked and rolled in flour and thrown in a pan of hot grease.

He was already filling his plate and he didn't have an answer for that.

At the table she said: I don't want you thinking the only reason you're here is so I'll have someone to feed my chickens. I always managed to get them fed and watered.

I don't mind doin it. A deal's a deal the way I see it.

We didn't have a deal. I always wanted a son. Albert and I weren't blessed with children, male or female. I don't claim to be able to take your parents' place but you're alone and since Albert was killed I've been alone myself. Seems to me as many people as there are in this world, a body ought to not be alone.

I got to where I didn't mind it, Yates said.

Really? Well I never. Daylong with no one to talk to and never hearing a human voice was too long for me.

No one to cook for and it didn't matter what time you did anything. It got to where it seemed like all I lived for was to keep the stock fed. People need a routine in their lives. Order.

Though he didn't admit, even to himself, the work served the purpose of forcing order on the formlessness of his own days. It gave him a sense of purpose that in the days to come became dear to him. With the cattle fed and in their stalls and the chickens basking in the heat and the house shuttered and closed down against the bitter night there was a comfort and a sense of security he'd never known. There'd be a cheery fire in the living room from the heating stove and the fireplaces in the bedrooms and at night he'd look at magazines or listen to the radio. Paiton had owned a Delco generator that provided electric lights and power for the electric icebox and he felt he'd stumbled blind into the tall cotton.

Somewhere sometime someone had made an error in the bookkeeping. He'd been deprived of the basic comforts folk take for granted and when the error had been discovered the coffers simply overflowed. He had money for the asking and a suit of clothes fit to be buried in and food anytime there were even intimations of hunger. There was a smokehouse and a food pantry stacked with jarred fruits and vegetables and jellies and preserves and she casually served up meals everyday that he'd have thought reserved for Sundays or holidays. Soft beds to sleep in and hot water for bathing and she seemed to take all this as no more than their due.

Still there was a vein of unease that ran through a faultline of pain, nagging as a toothache. As if he was taking too much of the world's largesse to him, no longer at one with the world, surviving on its own terms. He feared getting soft, ultimately unable to survive in the Spartan niche of life he'd carved for himself. There were moments when he was afraid he was an actor playing a part, a prostitute selling something of himself for three square meals and a feather bed. Promising something he was fundamentally unable to deliver. Now we don't want to be buyin somethin we can't pay for, he cautioned himself.

Nights by the fire she'd read to him Biblical tales. The stories of the stern old prophets, their mad ravings and rantings. Folk that had little given to them, little of compromise. Focused old graybearded men with their fierce onetrack minds and dire oratory. I bet them was some hardankled old sons of bitches, he told himself, and grinned when he thought of old Moses's drastic revision of Exodus.

She'd temper this with Twain, a chapter a night of Huckleberry Finn, Jim and Huck in flux on the sunrimpled Mississippi. He could almost smell the hot torpor of the river, seeing the country sliding past, until he was hopelessly snared by Twain, forced to seek out the book in surreptitious moments during the day, finish the book far ahead of her though she pretended not to notice and went on reading his chapter a night anyway.

It's the greatest novel an American ever wrote, she told him. She thought a while. Or any other nationality, she added.

There was something about her that reminded him vaguely of Crowe, and one night she admitted that she had once been the teacher at the Allen's Creek school.

I was just a girl, she said. A young foolish girl and I thought I could educate the world singlehandedly. Later I found I couldn't even educate Allen's Creek. The iron boom passed once the furnaces shut down and folks moved their children out of school and to other mining communities. They didn't have any use for a school. They wanted bootleg whiskey and a place to lose their money playing poker. Last time I went up Owl Hollow to look at the old schoolhouse the porch had caved in and there was a walnut tree growing through the roof. Folks had stolen the windows and they plundered the desks. I guess for kindling wood.

She fell silent, her eyes focused inward, and he thought she might be seeing the foolish redhaired girl she'd been, and wondering where she'd gotten herself to these years.

I seem to be overrun with schoolteachers here lately, he said.

What?

My friend Crowe. He used to be a schoolteacher in Maury County. He went to college and everything. He had a diploma but he burnt it. He said he had it in his head anyway.

I never knew he was a teacher. Or a black that could even read or write. He seems to be a peculiar man. Always to himself.

He minds his own business but he won't take nothin off of nobody.

I would think that would be an uncomfortable position for a black person to be in, she said. She fell silent again. After a time she said: or a person of any color, for that matter.

It was a bitter cold winter and he had little cause to regret his newfound station in life. The mire of offal and straw and earth in the cowlot froze hard as hoofmarked stone.

His boots rang hollowly on its whorled surface. He'd straighten from throwing down bales of hay from the loft and study the sky. It was slate gray and seemed to have been for months as if the weather had somehow become locked in this mode. Even as he watched through his frozen exhalation, a storm formed and exited the hollow as if the dark cove of bared branches was a repository of frozen turbulence, the progenitor of all storms. The snowflakes approached, driven by the wind, a slant and silent plague of ice. Behind it blue dusk, the world sinking into still cold water. He scrambled down and cut the seagrass twine, turning once to glance toward the house where she'd lit a lamp and a square of warm yellow light glowed like a beacon.

Inside it was warm. She fed him pork chops and potatoes and little green peas, apple pie for dessert and more creamy sweet milk than a man could drink.

You're a good boy, she told him. He shoveled up peas under his benign smile.

If the fireplace could not defeat the winter it could at least hold it at bay.

Night. Sleet sang against the glass. The room was warm. He had the covers drawn about his chin. Cozy as a grandfather badger dozing in his winter den deep in the earth. He listened to the wind outside, a man might perish in such cold. He thought of his existence before the widow Paiton claimed him, living in the woods, in the winds, housed only by whatever walled the world. Half asleep he thought of her. He thought of her white naked body laid the length of his own. Her breath on his throat. After a time, he slept the dreamless sleep of the weary and the righteous. Winter muttered balefully through the trees, raked fingernails of ice against the windows. They let him be.

On the way to Dow Cook's store there was a narrow swinging bridge slung between two trees in flimsy defiance of gravity and under his feet the frozen planking popped and slapped in a tintinnabulation of imminent doom so that he clung to the icy cables cautiously as if the whole thing might cascade from beneath his feet and plummet headlong into the waters below him.

Here was a bend in Allen's Creek and where he guessed the water was slowed for the curve, thin reefs of white ice had crept outward from the banks toward the center, the cold here merciless and implacable. Delicate lacework of ice that broke away with the current and potentially began to freeze the moving water again.

He climbed carefully down the laddered scaffolding and went on down the red road to the settlement. The day was frozen and silent and still. Nothing moved, not an animal, not a bird, not a leaf.

At Dow's he drank a dope and contested with the old loungers for a space around the coal stove. The air was hot and stale and smelled of chewing tobacco and smoke, the acrid smell of old men's sweat, a curious undercurrent he couldn't identify, the indefinable and somehow comfortable smell of time.

Make a hole for a cash customer, Yates said, holding the dope aloft and trying to force his way into the tight circle of warmth. You old codgers don't never even buy a dope. Sit in here and spit. I bet you bring your dinner and this a grocer store.

There's widow Paiton's housepet, one of the old men said sourly. Reckon does he bite? You reckon she's housebroke him yet?

I doubt it, another said. He's so used to shittin in the woods, I spect she has to collar and chain him up at night just to keep him in the house.

She could collar and chain me without too much of a fight, the first one said. She's a right smart of a good lookin woman. From a girl on she was more than Paiton ever deserved.

Well she's makin up for it now, old man Breece said. I reckon things balance themselves out. She's wound up with this fine outstanding young feller you see here.

Yates was far better off than anyone here and he knew it. There were folks here with nowhere to go when Dow's closed save singleboxed shanties lined with pasteboard, houses where even the rats shivered and hugged themselves, houses not designed for weather such as this, houses where you had to break ice in the bucket to get a drink of water.

The old men fell to complaining of the cold. The thermometer beside the store's front door hung at three degrees below zero nor would it move. The old men declared it frozen.

It ain't moved in a week, Breece said. I've been tryin to get Dow to bring it in by the heater and thaw it out but he's afraid it'll ruin it.

This cold about got me, Cates Hinson said. I've burnt everything fit to burn and I'm down to sayin this chair, or that one over there. I'm runnin out of chairs. How much heat do you reckon a grouchy stringyheaded old woman would put out?

Dow Cook would half listen to these endless conversations and interject his rallies at appropriate moments. Now he said: Mine ain't put out none in years, winter or summer, and waited for the dry halfhearted paperhusk chuckles.

Yates knew he was better off but he was careful not

to rub it in, a cautious decorum kept him downgrading his circumstances.

It ain't all steak and apple pie, he protested. Who you think feeds them damn hayburnin cows twice a day and breaks the ice to tote water to them?

How old are you boy?

I'm fifteen and a half.

Fifteen and a half. Shitfire. And livin in a house with a woman like that. There's folks livin in the world could be dipped in shit and sprout wildroses head to toe.

She's bein a real mother to me, Yates said piously.

One late winter day he went with a group of these men to check on a drunk named Old Man Teet. This was the only name he seemed to have. There was an undercurrent of uneasiness to them, a taste of dire foreknowledge that drew him like a magnet draws iron filings and he lagged along behind. They would singlefile up a hillside of frozen timber to where a shack perched happenstantial as a fallen leaf and, sure enough, Old Man Teet had frozen to death. He'd frozen on the dirt floor in an attitude of sleep save his eyes were open. He'd a bent arm beneath his head for a pillow and his shock of silver white hair spilled over it. His knees were pulled nigh to his chest in a fetal position and his free hand clutched a halfpint bottle to his stomach as if he'd drawn heat from it by sheer convection. Something in the frozen unflinching eyes made Yates turn his own eyes somewhere else.

Least he went out the way he was happiest, Breece said. Drunk as a bicycle and the bottle still half full. None of the old men said anything. Their breath plumed fragile and temporary as smoke.

He pried the frozen gray fingers from about the bottle. Raised it against the slategray sky as if he'd check for impurities. Apparently satisfied, he drank, his warted throat working. He wiped his mouth backhanded and shuddered and passed the bottle up to the other men. I expect that's the first Teet ever give anybody a drink of whiskey, he said. Most of the men passed the bottle on undrank from. They had to pry him loose from the greedy earth as if it were already claiming him and he came up frozen grotesquely stiff, pathetic yet somehow darkly halfcomical. By whatever appendage they could get a grip on, the old men tore him away. The corpse was an ungainly and unbalanced burden borne by old men scarcely less fragile than Teet himself. He looked like some arcane piece of furniture they were tugging or yet a curious plaything designed for the terminally demented they were fighting over. Give a hand here boy, Breece called. What little breath he had wheezed in his throat.

Yates looked back, his eyes drawn to Teet's erstwhile bed. Something cold he couldn't put a name to touched him. A handful of Teet's hair had been pulled out when they lifted him, and silver strands of hair each seized in the frozen earth as if the old man had been putting out roots.

Yates among the anointed, wearing a shirt of offwhite domestic the widow Paiton has sewn him and one of Albert Paiton's black ties. A suitcoat too big through the shoulders and with sleeves that hung halfway down his hands. The widow too was in Sunday raiment. They came afoot, winding down through the wildwood with other worshipers stringing out of the bare winter landscape, ascending into the glade of bare beeches where the clapboard church sits. Yates and the widow Paiton arrived with a mottled kind of dignity that rested uneasily on Yates's shoulders. A young squire and his lady perhaps, or country scion of old generation to generation aristocracy gone to seed. The church is like a church of myth or fairytale. It is crept with ivy and, even in the early spring, the air smells like honeysuckle.

Not inside. Inside the air is cold and cloistral and unforgiving. It seems unwilling to concede an inch. It smells of old polished wood and musty hymnals and angry righteousness.

Stiff and decorous, the soured rustle of the pages of ancient text, voices lift in song, *Come, come, come to the church in the wildwood.* Yates might sing along but he doesn't know the words. The widow Paiton holds the songbook closer for him to see but he can smell the musky femininity of her, and his head swims and the words slither off the page like serpents and he wants gone, somewhere else, the creekbank, the dark woods, anywhere. He studied one of the pictures in the hymnal in a kind of awed silence. The painting showed a graveyard stricken with an orgy of turmoil, tombstones toppling, graves exploding in clods of flying earth and spraying dirt. The sky was full of previously entombed folk bound upward with arms outstretched like divers unaffected by gravity or capeless funeralclad superheroes ascending skyward.

The Reverend Meecham paces the raised platform before the pulpit like a mad bear. Front and back, left to right, front and back, his strides measure the boundaries of whatever confines him. This preacher dressed himself always in black and with his large mournful eyes and in these dusky cerements he had much the appearance of a scorched owl and there even hovered about him always the odor of singed cloth and hair as if he'd come too close to the fires of torment and managed to jerk himself away from the flames by the thinnest of margins.

His voice raised in a strident tirade against wickedness. A wickedness generic and unspecific, but a kind of one size fits all sin that's crouched beyond these churchhouse walls. Its tendrils have crept to the sills and through, there is no soul here not touched by evil. Little hope is held out for the folk clustered here. He rants on like one demented, the electric air before him a fog of spittle and even so hardshelled a soul as Yates's becomes a little qualmy. Shitfire, he thinks. He knows hell like he was born and brought up there. There is a little reward promised here but to escape the molten eternal torment he so lovingly describes seems paradise enough.

In a lull of this verbal storm, at length, Meecham ran a trembling hand across his bouffant teased hair and began to call for souls. Everything that transpired seemed to have been geared to bring this moment about. The air in the church house had grown close and stifling and Meecham was wet with sweat. Get up here and own up, he calls. Tell what it was you done and let God decide what's goin to happen to you.

To Yates's eye there seemed to be a rush to be first. Folk arise and struggle toward the pulpit, there seemed no soul here so poor it does not possess its own sin and the will to proclaim it.

Of a sudden the man in the pew in front of Yates was taken by a sort of fit. He began to jabber wildly in some language Yates had never heard spoken and to jerk and shudder in a curious epileptic dance. He turned toward Yates, his legs jittering so crazily, you'd think each independent. He was a redfaced man in faded overalls and his eyes were crude and staring and profoundly vacant, seeing not Yates but through Yates to some sere landscape flickering with fire and roiled with sulfur smoke through which the vague shapes of demons moved covertly on their dark appointed rounds.

Jesus, he began to shriek in a rising crescendo. Their madness seemed wildly communicable, for others took up the cry and some fell to the floor kicking and clawing and rolling about perpetually calling upon Jesus and more yet began to run from one side of the church to the other and back, veering crazily off the walls and leaping pews, arms flapping gracelessly like birds constrained to the earth so that Yates began to fear for his safety. He straightened from his seat with an eye cast for the door. The widow would restrain him but he shook off her hand.

He'd struggled through and sometimes across jerking apoplectic bodies to the end of the aisle when an enormous woman careened off him and slammed him backward hard into a pew and cracked his elbow on the hardwood flooring. Lights flickered behind his eyes. He sat and rubbed his elbow painfully. You're crazy as shit, he screamed after her but she had veered off into the turmoil of rampant salvation and was momentarily lost from sight. When she reappeared she seemed to be bearing down upon him again but he was up and running. He was knocked down twice and once drawn into the embrace of some lecherous old Lazarus before he made the door but when he did he slammed it and stood leaning against it as if he'd confine all this madness within until it burned itself out. Then, after a time, he went and sat on the church house steps and listened to the shrieks and the bumps and

thumps of furniture being thrown about. His tie was crazily askew and someone had jerked on one end of it and
halfchoked him. One of the buttons had been ripped off
the domestic shirt. Beneath the dark black coat he was
wet with sweat and he was half crying from the hot throb
of his elbow.

He had a thought for the widow Paiton and what
might befall her needs but she'd made this bed and he
figured to just let her lie in it.

He thought of what she'd told him about heaven. If
it's run by this crazy bunch of shitasses she can have two
portions of it, hers and mine both, he thought.

He guessed he'd just take his chances.

Midweek he was sitting on the bottom step of the company store porch with an Orange Crush between his feet
when Clyde Spears climbed up beside him.

Hey Yates. I seen you at church Sunday.

Say you did? Well you won't again.

Yates drank from his orange and set the bottle back
down. Them son of a bitches is crazy. Church my ass.
They ought to just change the sign and make it a crazy
house.

I seen you leavin early.

Well. I never was one for growin old but I would like
to see twentyone. That goddamned Sursee woman run flat
over me and was lookin to do it again. She done it apur-
pose too.

She was just taken hard by the spirit.

She was taken hard by somethin. All of them sons of

a bitches was.

Spears sat down on the next step up and began to roll a Country Gentleman cigarette. Yates stared bemusedly at the road. Across the bend in the creek he could see the ruined furnaces rearing out of the honeysuckle and three brick flue furnaces towering dizzily against it like monoliths remarking some order that no longer existed in this world or another. From beyond the dense trees there was the perpetual dull clang of the rock crusher, a noise so palpable it was almost visible, above it the fierce blue sky wavered electrically.

There was several souls taken Sunday.

I know another one they're fixin to get. Some old man grabbed me around the neck and kissed me on the jaw and if I ever catch that son of a bitch out I aim to lay him flat with a firebrick.

Spears was sniggering to himself then he fell to coughing. He ground the cigarette out beneath a booted foot. When he quit coughing he said: I reckon you're just doomed for torment.

I reckon so.

Least you know where you stand. Leavin early like you done you missed some good confessions. I always go just for them. No tellin what you're liable to hear when they're taken by the Holy Ghost and cryin to get right with God. It's bettern a newspaper. I remember one time Leonard Fain confessed to screwing old man Tippydo's wife while she was cookin Tippydo's breakfast. Said she never quit rollin out biscuits.

I don't care about any of that news. I just wanted gone.

Widow Paiton repented too. You missed that.

What in the world would she have to repent for? I thought she was holier than thou.

Spears sniggered again. She's done it two or three times. She said she had lust in her heart.

Say she has.

Spears arose. He dusted flakes of tobacco off his overalls. Got to git on, he said. Got to go fore I'm sent for.

Yates didn't hear him. He was making interlocking circles in the planking with the cold wet bottle.

She didn't say who it was she had it for did she? he asked.

That warm spring, dreams came to trouble his sleep. His sleep was no longer the tranquil guiltless sleep of his childhood. Playful erotic nymphs, faceless, all soft breaths and hot vaginas covered with hair that were stranger than any dreams he'd known and were not faces of past folk he'd known or old events replayed like other dreams but nymphs conjured by his mind out of sheer ectoplasm, sweet slow languorous dreams that split to gossamer tatters with the opening of his eyes and left him with only shards of sweetly pornographic memory that were already fading in the morning, as he clasped himself beneath the sweaty sheets thinking he couldn't stand it, a fierce and a hot aching tumescence and a gnawing fear for his sanity.

The widow Paiton's dreams were troubled as well. Old memories, old feelings from her girlhood came to haunt her. Old suitors she'd picked through and cast aside, dancing and music from a long time ago, the smell of summer flowers.

She never dreamed of Paiton.

She dreamed of the black angus bull Paiton had bought, arrogant and enormously masculine, stalking the hall of the barn like a predator. She dreamed of the sunlight on his rippling ebony hide.

Gradually in a series of tangled dreams the bull became a man. The man had no face but he had a color and that color was black. A dark satyr that taunted her and stroked her breasts with hands the color of old walnut. She dreamed of phallic thrusts that were hard as blows struck in anger and awoke in hot breathless dark with her loins freshened and nipples taut.

She would pray. She'd sleep again and the dream would always be waiting, the shadowy succubus with a phallus as hard and cold as ice and she'd awaken and pray again. She could call forth the Reverend Meecham's face before hers reproachful and accusing but the satyr paid it no mind. She tried to call forth the face of God but this visage was so unreckonable that she was utterly lost and tears would stain her face.

Had winter lasted forever perhaps he would have remained cradled in the warm care of the widow Paiton but all things pass and this was not to be. Ultimately the ice began to thaw. The snow began to melt and run off the roof all day. He could hear its steady drip throughout the night and all the world seemed perpetually adrip. The barnyard went to a sea of sucking black mud and the wind shifted to the south and came looping up out of the hollow, soft as a promise.

That spring there were nights when the house simply would not contain him. The rich odors of the night would drift in. He'd be up and gone through window or door whichever he came upon first not caring if she missed him or not. He'd just let the night take him.

The night was rich and humid and rampant with growth and a kind of uncontrollable sexuality. The night was a compound of odors, the rich black odor of the turned humus, the thickening greenery, a sweet compound of honeysuckle and attar of rose and cool damp green smell of the night itself, a world unexplored that was his alone to do with as he chose, an infinity of possibilities he could bend to his will.

He wandered far into these nights and he had no thought for sleep or need for it. Sleep was something other folks needed, he had transcended it without even meaning to. The fecund spring nights sang in his blood like wine. Couched in the boughs of an enormous beech he'd listen to the shanties fall silent, eavesdropping on the world at large, making it part of his life whether it wanted him or not, and watching the last of the yellow windows sucked down to darkness and sleep taking the ruined settlement as the last ones left burning were dictated by the rituals of sickness or death or courtship.

On the bluff by the river near one of his old haunts, he watched a spring storm following the stream like opposites attracting, fire to water. Tracking tendrils of black clouds toward the surface of the river like smoke from whatever the storm combusted. Lightning fierce and staccato, burning out of absolute nothingness, the slant and windy rain blowing downriver faint and fainter, the pale willows shivering, thunder dimming, finally honing away thinly to nothingness, ultimately only a faroff rosecolored flickering beneath the metallic clouds. Scattered among the rocks lay translucent eggs of hail, glowing dimly as if they held some unfathomable light of their own. Like a gift from some wilder and simpler time when nothing existed save the elements.

Another night there was music, timeless and so sourceless he might have dreamed it. *I'm way down in jail on my knees*, a black voice sang, *way down in jail on my knees*. A bottleneck guitar played notes that seemed to him sadder than anything he'd ever heard, a music so sad and mournful it was past all transcending, save by the ear or by the heart, awakening in him a bleak and tender desire. *Going where the climate suits my clothes, lord goin where the climate suits my clothes*.

By then he was part of the night. You could not separate the two, he felt if you jerked him away from the night now, one of the two would bleed, he was as at home in it as the whippoorwills he startled that rose over him with dark wings enormous and eyes glowing red as rubies in the moonlight.

Far up Allen's Creek at some hour beyond all clocking, he came upon a swimming hole like a pool from some old halfforgotten legend, gleaming in the starlight like pooled mercury.

Halted by the soft murmurs of a courting couple, he knelt in the dewy grass watching. Like dreamimages the two lovers disrobed and waded into the water. He could see the pale bloom of her breasts, the dark smudge of hair beneath her rounded stomach. Hear their soft laughter, secretive, private, remaining so for all his watching. When they walked out of the water, their wet bodies were grailed with faint starlight and they touched and sank to the dewy grass of one accord as if drawn there by something past their control and, when they coupled, the white bodies seemed simply to collapse one into the other with a grave decorum unlike anything he'd seen from coupling beasts and he just kept watching in a kind of stricken wonder.

There were times when he'd wonder: Am I crazy? He'd have had to answer: I don't know.

With the awl he worked the hole larger. Then Yates leaned to peer one-eyed through it. It was amazing the view the hole afforded once you put your eye to it. He'd studied it from the underside of the bathroom ceiling and it was scarcely noticeable. You had to know it was there.

He laid the awl aside and looked again. He could see the entire top surface of the bathtub, a great expanse of white porcelain the color of old ivory. He waited. It was warming up in the attic and it was dark when he looked away from the lighted bathroom. He could smell old suncured wood, the baking tin roof, hear the drone of dirtdaubers plying their craft. The tin popped under the weight of the sun. Somewhere off toward the barn there was the crowing of a cock. He waited with an air of impatience. Had he possessed a watch he would have looked at it.

When at length he heard her step in the hallway and the opening of the bathroom door, he fixed an eye to the hole again. He heard the bathroom door close and the bolt slide home and he had a thought for how impotent that latch was.

He still couldn't see anything save the tub. He heard

the widow moving about in motions that sounded curiously furtive and he heard the sound of a zipper and the soft whisper of fabric against fabric. He waited. A white disembodied arm reached across the tub. It stoppered the tub. It turned the water on, waited to test how hot it was. It disappeared. He watched water run for awhile. His knees began to ache.

His interest quickened when a leg stepped into the tub. Then he could see the pale expanse of her back, smooth and slightly dusted with freckles. The shoulderblades rippled beneath the flesh. He scarcely breathed. Then she lay on back with her knees drawn up and he could see her white pooled breasts and mounded stomach and the thick thatch of red hair below it and her long ivory thighs. Her eyes were closed. Slowly she began to soap herself. He'd never noticed how long and tapering her fingers were. Soaped her breasts, her armpits, the length of her thighs. When her hand crept up her inner thigh and hesitated where the flesh folded it was all he could do to keep from crying out. He fumbled open his clothing and clasped himself.

Of a sudden there was a dry shriek of protesting nails being torn from wood and the entire four by eight section of ceiling board he was crouched on listed. The front dropped away from the joists and listed further then plummeted floorward with Yates riding like some magic-carpeted Aladdin. Some perverse fairytale Aladdin with jeans hobbled about his knees and mouth agape and white eyes rolled wide in sheer unalloyed horror and an enormous erection clasped before him bothhanded like some weapon he'd do battle with.

He slammed into the sink and the sheetrock shattered and his head slapped the wall so hard the room went electrically white. He was up immediately trying to haul up his breeches and kick broken sheetrock out of his way, but she was up from the tub, up with an outraged garbled shriek, all bobbing breasts and dripping pubic hair and ivory stomach, unmindful of her nakedness and flailing him about the head with whatever fell to hand, brushes, a bottle of shampoo, her fists. You little beast, she began to yell. You filthy little beast.

She was staying between him and the door but he went under a restraining arm and got a hand on the knob and tried to turn it. It wouldn't turn. While he fumbled for the thumbbolt then threw it, she was slamming him with a bar of soap. He went through the screen door at a dead run with a tide of invective rising behind him and the door slammed and rocked on its spring. By the time he'd reached the barn he had adjusted his clothing and calm had overtaken him. There appeared to be no pursuit and he'd slowed his pace to one of dignified retreat. He crossed through the fence and went through a stand of sumac onto the red road. He looked back once at the house and there was a look on his face akin to regret for all that was lost to him.

A goodlookin widow woman takes you in and gives you a fine house to live in and feather beds to sleep in and God knows what else and what do you do? First thing you know you're back sleepin under bluffs and stealin chickens. How come you to do that anyway?

Yates would've died before he would have told Crowe. I don't like milkin cows, he said.

You don't like milkin cows? Boy you got to sort of work around and get you a hold on life. Try to make it do what you want it to instead of the other way around. If you don't, you goin be the bottom dog all your life. You ain't old enough to join the Army.

I'm old enough to die.

That night he slept in a cedar grove where owls called all night. The cedars must have been thick with whip-poorwills for he went to sleep to their crying and when he woke before the first gray light they were crying still. With day they ceased but no songbirds commenced. All there was of sound was doves calling forlornly from some dark hollows. A bedlam of their calls all above him as if he'd chosen to sleep in the epicenter of a community of doves. It turned colder in the night. In the morning when he went out the world had frozen. A light rain was falling but it was freezing on the trees and each leaf, each twig, each blade of grass was seized in a delicate caul of ice. The trees clashed softly with the wind. Ice had frozen in a mud hole and he leant to study it. Milkcolored ice in a design of marvelous intricacy, risen above the level of water itself and frozen whitely in mid-air like some magical construction for elves or fairies, freezing pure white out of the frozen mud and suspended over it gossamerlike. He tapped it gently with a fingernail and it broke with the sound of a small forlorn chime. He went and sat on the south face of the bluff waiting for the sun but when it came there was only a wan suffusion of light and no warmth. He sat hugging himself and waiting for the day to warm, but it did not.

It was early May and should have been past the last

of the cold spells the old men tirelessly catalogued as dog-
wood winter, blackberry winter. They didn't have a name
for this one and over at Dow Cook's store, they argued
back and forth. Toad frog winter, whippoorwill winter and
ultimately it was left unnamed as some freakish aberration
of the weathers.

As the week progressed, it did not warm and Yates
had fallen to work dragging piles of leached out stumps and
dead treetops to burn at night. On the fourth night it came
a killing frost and Yates by his bonfire watched it form all
around him in the air, minute crystals of ice appearing out
of nothing and gleaming in the still cold air like powdered
glass settling slowly to the earth. It was something few
men had seen and apprehensively he judged it some kind
of warning. He'd angered the gods, or whoever's hand was
at the tiller of the world and given rules no longer applied.

The woods were full of ripe rampant greenery killed
by the frost. In the days that followed, hot weather returned
and the trees and flowers and bushes fermented and soured
and rotted and the air was full of their briny reek. In the
white sun the forest steamed and smoked in a shifting mist
like some vast carboniferous forest in a fable of when the
world was new. Or yet some world whose caretakers had
grown bored or distracted, who'd given up in midseason
and turned away to something else, this world forgotten or
given up on, tired of the delicate and unending administra-
tion to flower and leaf and sparrow.

He knocked and waited awhile. He turned to watch water stringing off the metal of the porch. Beyond lay bleak

fields, a barn, a line of cedar trees. He knocked again. He could hear someone stirring inside the house. He was wearing a black wool watchcap and he removed it and stood turning it nervously in his hands.

The door opened. A woman was regarding him with a calm placid face. Her eyes were blue and a stray hair curled toward the left one. Her skin was smooth and pore-less as a china cup.

Yes? she said.

I reckon you sent for me, he said.

She studied his face. He'd said it as if she'd sent for him yesterday, the day before.

Yes, she said. I reckon I did. She pushed the door wider. You get on in here where it's warm. How many nights did you come?

Two or three. Four maybe. I throwed little rocks against your window glass and thought you'd know what it meant.

Well. I'm sorry, I guess I reckon I'm a little slow. I ought to have put two and two together. Any fool ought to know from a tap on her window that you want her to come out and talk awhile.

The sun that summer was fierce and merciless. The heat hung in the hot windless dark long after the sun had set. The heat and the unceasing noise of the crusher and the bewildering succession of days, one the same as the oth-er, settled in the hollows like a plague. The hot smoky coal oil darkness was tinged with doom. Night came but it brought no relief. They slept in the troubled and exhausted sleep of the drugged and awoke into a malefic sun and a day so identical to the one preceding they might have been trapped in time like a fly in amber.

A mad dog summer maligns the heart. Tempers frayed and friends fell out and there was a fatal cutting on the evening shift at the crusher. Rumors of madness and hydrophobia, of things unchained to prowl the night, beasts that locked on to your spoor and tracked you as tireless as fates. Husbands and wives took to eyeing each other speculatively across the supper table and going to bed in uneasy silence and when Clarence Pedigo's wife eased barefoot back into the house with her lover's semen still hot inside her and pulled the screen door softly to and raised a hand to smooth a sweatdampened curl out of her eyes the room went electrically bright and in the shotgun's concussion she was blown backward through the door she'd so soundlessly closed in a summer storm of blood and shattered wood and a sudden windswept silence that felt like a shout.

Somewhere glass broke and he whirled. An old woman was turning from an empty milkjug she'd dropped and was hurrying back toward the gate. The widow Paiton was trying to struggle out of his embrace. Mrs. Cook, she called once loudly but the old woman didn't even glance back. If anything, she increased her gait. The widow Paiton quit struggling and pillowed her face in his throat and began to cry and he thought for one dislocated crazy moment that she was crying because the milkjug was broken or because the old woman wouldn't come back and then the enormity of what had happened hit him like a hammerblow.

Her bare breast was still free of her clothing, milkwhite, exposed and forbidden. He looked across the woman's russet head to where the old woman was. She was almost through the gate and she was running toward the road. He clasped her breast with his hand. Alabaster white dusted with russet freckles the way he had known it would be and he thought his hand looked like a great black malignant spider clamped there feeding at her teat. He turned his face to hers and pulled aside the strands of auburn hair at her throat and kissed her lightly below the ear and was gone.

They were strung out at the mouth of Paiton Hollow, fanning out from the ridge above the Muledick and cresting on the old wagon log road that led to the openpit mine, a dozen men or more, some with kerosene lanterns held thighhigh before them, scanning the brush and all encumbered by weapons that normally served more agrarian functions and a gun or two among them and one with a coil of rope. Yates could hear faroff voices calling flickering one to the other and he could see lights through the timber. They seemed to be in search of someone. Always glancing over his shoulder and always expecting pursuit from one quarter or another he assessed what might cause all this commotion.

He was coming down the road and they were coming up with such stealth that when he rounded the curve he was almost upon them. He glanced about, he seemed to know their faces, but tonight there was something different about them. His first impulse was to whirl and run but they all seemed to see him at once and before he could flee they'd sauntered up out of the brush.

Dow Cook was one of them who had a gun. He carried a newlooking lantern as some of the others did and Yates guessed they'd been outfitted from the company store. Dow raised the lantern so close to Yates's face he could feel the heat, smell the hot smoky coaloil.

Instinctively he stepped backward from the hot lantern but Dow just advanced upon him and the men gathered about him in a loose circle.

Where you been? Dow asked.

Yates mouth was already open to say: What's it to you? But something in the storekeeper's face or voice stopped him.

Just out on the ridge, he said.

If you was out the part of ridge your nigger running mate lives on I guess you found more than you figured on. Where's he at?

Who?

Don't play the fool with me, niggerlover. Where's he at?

Dow Cook laid the axehandle across his throat and pushed hard enough for the pressure to constrict his windpipe. He couldn't swallow and he couldn't breathe. He tried to twist away. Dow's breath was foul, as if he'd been feasting on the dead.

Where's he at? You know where the black son of a bitch is and you're goddamned well goin tell it.

He couldn't breathe. He balled his fist and struck downward hard and slammed Dow's solar plexus and Dow's lungs emptied in a foetid expulsion and the axe fell away. Dow's face went past his own almost in slow-motion like the image of a face in a film receding and he struck it as hard as he could feeling the lip split rubbery and a broken tooth lacerate his knuckle. He went literally over Dow's limp body into a wall of men with torches and tools flailing at him. They were not like actual men but simply a wall of appendages and clutching hands trying to clasp and drag him down. He came out of them running on his hands and knees scrambling wildly up like a fallen deer already running before it was erect and heading for the trees.

He went full tilt between the dark boles of trees running shadow to shadow and little more than a fleeting shadow himself, running panicked and blind through a night gone telluric and electric, something strange abroad in the night that touched him with desperation and sent him halfsliding down steep slopes and leaping recklessly into darkness and guided only by the memories of places seen by daylight.

More skilled or perhaps just desperate, he was soon far from any pursuit he could hear. When he eased through a stand of sumac at the border of the road he did so cautiously but the only light he could see was far down the road and then passed from sight in a curious torchlit procession into the trees. He went on toward the furnaces. He'd come out a quartermile or so up from the store and he went on toward it, saved from certain destruction solely by blind luck.

Where the brush climbed and thickened and beyond where he knew the road ran he stopped and stood breathing hard with his hands on his knees. His side was stitched with pain and sweat was fairly running off him. He thought he was going to be sick but all that came up was a mouthful of hot bitter bile and he staggered on.

I know a place but don't stop to pack no bag, they all around everywhere, Yates told him.

Crowe was wildeyed and shaking. His ebony face was slick and shiny and as poreless as a museum likeness wrought from mahogany. His clothes were wet where he'd forded some stream or where he'd sweated through them and there was a sour reek of sweat about him, like the taste of a cankered penny, as if Crowe had been sweating the very essence of fear itself. The wild frightened musk of some beast finally brought up short at the end of the hunt, cornered by dogs and waiting for the kill.

He sat hunkering in the honeysuckle and he seemed to be making a visible effort to compose himself. Water beaded and ran off his face. He fetched up from the pocket of his shirt a pack of Luckies and shook one out and sat clutching it between his fingers. He sat so for a time as if he'd forgotten it. The cigarettes were soaked and the one he held bent limply and water dripped from the end of it.

After a time he said, you got a light?

Yates was looking at the cigarette. He shook his head. You couldn't light that thing with a blowtorch, he said.

God almighty, Crowe said. Where the hell is this place. How did you find it?

Yates snickered, I was brought up just down the road from here. No tellin what kind of freaks of nature might be in here. Eyeless fish. Titless mermaids.

Crowe shook his head. Sometimes I think you're crazy and other times I just know you are.

The store was locked. He simply went around to the side and threw a brickpot through the window and cleared the loose shards of glass out of the frame and climbed in.

As a shopper he could have browsed at his leisure but he moved up the aisles of tabled merchandise in haste and he scarcely saw what he was loading into his poke. Tinned Vienna sausages and beans, little flat cans of sardines. Moon Pies and what looked like enough varied provender for a week. He'd hoped for better luck, but even when fleeing an impromptu lynch party Yates's business sense had prevailed. On his way out he found a dusty box of flashlights and shoved one in a hip pocket. He was already out the window and outward bound when he stopped and set everything down and went back. He'd used all his matches and he was feeling in the dark by the time he found the batteries.

Small felon couched in the rank weeds with his plunder about him, hastily assembling the flashlight and cupping the lens with a palm, then clicking it on to see did it work.

It did. He took up the bag and hurried off.

He came playing the light across the black waters of the

lake but if another side existed it requires more light than this to see it. The light faded out across the glassflat waters. The light flickered upward then where a bulbous ceiling black as obsidian gleamed wetly. Crowe looked away, to nothing. He didn't like the place. This antiplace. Something about the light tending to nothing made him dizzy.

The boy came up proffering the bag. Crowe took it. Yates was playing the light into the bag, turning up this item, that item. I didn't know what your favorites was but I probably got it covered. Seems like I got a little of everything.

Crowe hardly noticed. You see anybody?

I reckon I seen about everbody. The woods is full of em, it's a wonder they ain't lynching one another. Dow Cook like to cut my throat with a axehandle but he's been lookin to do it anyway. He ain't never liked me.

That's hard to believe, Crowe said. Somebody that ain't never liked you.

I notice he ain't never had you over for Sunday dinner. Ain't named none of his kids after you neither.

How long you reckon I'll have to stay down here?

I don't know. Three or four days maybe. I'd come out one night and just ease off and keep on easin.

I may ease off quicker than that. I can't stand this damn place no three or four days. This son of a bitch just gives me the allovers.

I always thought you were tough, Yates said.

There's a difference between bein tough and just not givin a shit. Where does it go?

Go?

Where the hell does it go? It just spreads out and you can't see no end to it and it's pitchblack in here twenty-four hours a day.

I got some extra batteries.

Better let me have them then.

He fished up the batteries out of his jeans and Crowe took them, fed them one at a time into his pockets.

You get a can opener?

Why hell no. I knowed there was something else but I couldn't think what.

You still got that old knife?'

I always got it but I'd hate to lose it. I'd hate to not get it back.

Just let me have it a day or two.

Well. I guess you could leave it up there by the ladder. Leave it on that little shelf in the rock.

How about I leave it struck in Dow Cook's heart for you? You reckon you could find it there?

Yates didn't answer. Everything had turned strange and surreal, things were happening too fast. He'd seen Crowe burnt out, men he'd known all his life had attacked him with farm implements. There was something different about Crowe, something remote and coldblooded, distant and deadly in his voice. He reached him the knife. In the beam of the flashlight Crowe's gray hands took the knife, opened it. Yates noticed for the first time how clean and cared for Crowe's hands were, how meticulous he'd been about his person. Now he was crazed with mud and pigshit and the rank of sweat and his shirt was tattered by thornrose and he looked halfcrazy and bloody furrows had dried on him. Damned if you ain't crawled through a hogpen or somethin, Yates said. They'll figure you just headed out.

They may unless somebody tells them.

Hellfire. Nobody knows but us and I don't think you'll say anything.

Only a fool would trust another man completely. Or woman.

I trust you, Yates said, his fair head a nimbus of light.

Then you best grow out of it, Crowe said. I said anybody, friend or daddy or whatever. Things runs along smooth and everything's all right but when things get squally folks start to look out for theirselves. You're by yourself and you better be lookin over your shoulder. A man's born into the world a separate unit, by hisself and when he lays down at last to die he has to do that by hisself too. In between these two points there's an illusion of kinship but an illusion is all it is and don't be fooled by it. It don't take nothin to ruin it. Less than you'd think. A wrong word, the look on a face in a certain light, the wind. Then you're back on your own and poorer for the time you've wasted.

Crowe fell silent for a time. By the flashlight his face looked impassive and immobile, not a face at all then but a representation of a face carved from old dark wood, talismanic, ceremonial. The silence hung to a thin wire strung tight. Water was dripping somewhere at measured intervals as regular as a clock ticking.

Goddamn it Crowe, what? Yates asked.

They'd make you tell, he said. Or you'd decide to tell. You'd be a bigshot for a day or two. The boy who caught the nigger who raped the white woman. You see what I got to do.

I see you've gone as crazy as a shithouse mouse. You know me better than that. You got to.

At the very bottom of things you're white and I'm black, Crowe said. There was a dead dull weariness in his voice. He was clasping the knife loosely righthanded.

You couldn't do it.

I can do whatever I have to do. There's white men's bones covered with honeysuckle vines in an old cistern in Maury County. They didn't think I could do it either.

There was a curious helpless look in the eyes, but the abrupt click of the light took everything down to breathless darkness. Simultaneously Yates dropped to a crouch and backpedaled two steps with the whoosh, whoosh over his head of Crowe's arms making windmills to part the air. He dropped to the stone floor silently and rolled, fetched up sitting and shucking off his shoes. With the shoes clutched under an arm he struck off in the direction he thought the entrance lay.

Hey boy, Crowe screamed.

The sound came amplified and absolutely sourceless, from everywhere at once, from nowhere at all. It kept rolling wave on wave upon him till he stopped his ears, the dark calling him mockingly by name, boy, boy, boy.

Hey boy, can't you take a joke?

The voice was hollow and enormous, the voice of a jovial fairytale giant who ate boys, the walls booming joke, joke, joke.

He flicked the light once to affix the opening then immediately off again. When the light clicked on Crowe cried out somewhere near the water. He'd been going the wrong way. Yates heard him fall and swear.

When he was through the chasm he felt about for the pinch bar. He didn't even think about what he was doing. He began to pinch the tablet of stone across the opening, the only sound the click of the steel bar on stone, his ragged breathing. There was no sound or light beyond the stone door. When he was finished he laid the bar aside and he was surprised to discover that he was crying. He went cautiously up the chambered hallway to his lair where moonlight fell oblique and silver. Without pausing or so much as a look around, he went up the ladder toward it, his shadow and the ladder's shadow wavering inkblack against the pale limestone, his own shadow twisted and

curiously simian, like the shadow of some denizen of the
nether regions tentatively and for the first time ascending
to the world of light.

His stomach had twisted and shriveled and became as if
it were devouring itself but he guessed he ought to be glad
water was no problem. Water seeped and dripped everywhere and he had only to stop and listen. Above the rasp
of his labored breathing and the hammer blows of his heart
he could hear it falling everywhere and in this world of di-
minished, yet heightened senses, it seemed to ring on stone
like a hammer on steel. The dark seemed an unreckonable
enormity as if this lightless and watery firmament was an
antiworld of perpetual night couched below a world hol-
lowed and filled with water, a globe fissured and striated
with hairline cracks that threatened to inundate him, to
drown him in a black and soundless tidal surge down these
inkblack corridors to he knew not where.

Somewhere he had been once, he remembered that
the sun set and the sun rose but, for certain, there'd been
no evidence to the contrary. Here he had come to think
it always night. Deep in the heart of his perpetual night
he fell to his knees on the cold wet stone and clasped his
hands before him and closed his eyes and turned his face
upward toward impenetrable darkness.

Oh Lord, he began to pray. You've got to help me.
You've put me down here and clearlight forgot me. I know
it's been a while since I checked in but I'm here knockin
at your door now and you've advertised redemption and
forgiveness for the sins of man and I'm here to take ad-

vantage of your offer. It's powerful dark down here. It's darker than the inside of a black cat in this place, blacker than the heart of a Flatrock Baptist preacher. It's despair, darker than shit and I've got to have some relief.

There in the dark that was black beyond darkness and black beyond redemption and black even beyond the power of light to defray it, his unseen face twisted in self-mockery. The frozen rictus grin of a corpse. Harsh laughter shook him and his sides hurt and his shoulders jerked and tears rolled unchecked from his useless eyes.

I'll do whatever you want me to. Just tell me. Write the words in fire forty feet tall. I'll place my feet wherever you guide them. I'll give up all my material wealth and live among the heathen and show them the error of their ways and lead them toward the light like sheep on the path to your righteousness. I'll help old women across the street and lost children find their way home and if anybody badmouths you, I'll be on them with a flail pole like a cat on a rat but you've got to do your part. I've got to have some light down here. Man wasn't built to stand such a place and, in all honesty, I question your wisdom in even making such a fault in the earth. Did you do it and forget about it? Were you drunk? Did you do it on a bet? Well the joke's over. Enough is efuckin nuff. I want you to smite the peace with the mighty hammer of your fist and slam the top off of it and let your sweet clean light fall where it's never fell before and all that is unclean here shrivel and dry like a spider in the hot sun.

He wiped the tears away from his burning eyes with a sleeve. He could hear the rapid panting of his breath, hear the blood in his veins, he could smell his foulness. The reek of dried sweat and his stale fetid breath and smell of urine where he'd wet himself from sheer terror.

He got up leaning awkwardly as if braced for a stiff

leeward wind. I ask all this in Jesus's name amen, he said. He staggered off again and he couldn't have said if he'd been here before or this was someplace new to him and he thought of Yates saying: *I was brought up just down the road from here.* After awhile he could hear water running and he walked on toward it for the sheer relief from silence and the noise grew to a roar and the air was full of a cold mist of stinging spray. Before he knew it he was ankledeep in icy water and he stopped, veered instantly back for he had no inkling how deep these waters might be. He made to go around them but each time he advanced again he was in the water. He swung far to his right, hand on gradually rising rock and came up against a jagged bluff where he could hear the water cascading down from somewhere in the void above in a roar down the vertical wall of bluff and the pitch of this roar never changed as if this had been going on forever and would continue so when his very bones were dust.

Well fuck it, Crowe said aloud. He went down the grade and waded into the stream and almost instantly it was thighdeep and cold as ice. These be baptismal waters, he shouted. And if they take me so be it.

He went on cautiously easing his left foot out feeling the bottom, slick and unseen, but he drew a sparse comfort from the fact that there was bottom there at all. The water roiled about his chest and then his throat and he was on tiptoe fighting the current with his lips clinched tight against the water. Then the next step the water was back lapping at his chest and he breathed a sigh of relief guessing he'd crossed the deepest part. The next step there was no bottom to touch and he went under the black water with a silent outraged stream of bubbles and came up downstream gagging and spitting and fighting the water. He felt solid rock under him and the current turned him, rock again. He struck out swimming blindly for the shore, any shore, and beached breathless and shivering on a smooth shoreline of rock that rose gradually out of the waters and ascended who knew where. He rested a moment, his heart hammering, his breathing a thin ragged harsh rasp that was almost a sob. Then he began to pull himself slowly up the span of rock. He attempted once to stand but the rock was too slick and he half fell and he went then on his hands and knees like an animal. After awhile the rock wasn't wet anymore and he could keep his footing and he straightened and went up the rock.

When he could go no further without resting he stopped. He had been climbing for what seemed an immeasurable distance, an immeasurable time.

What I wouldn't give for a pack of Lucky Strikes, he said. I'd walk a mile for a Camel. His voice sounded at once hollow and amplified as if he were addressing unseen throngs in some vast amphitheater. Or even a sack of Country Gentleman, he said after awhile.

He guessed at least he was moving toward the surface of the earth. He had no way knowing how far down he had been or how high up he had to go or what would be there when he arrived. For all he could do was put one foot in front of the other. His footsteps rang hollowly on stone. In his mind he was climbing an ornate staircase of a great vast round coliseum abandoned eons ago and far above his head an enormous vaulted ceiling hundreds of feet away. The stairway wound upward toward the ceiling and below him the earth was dizzily far away. The staircase swayed and creaked and drifted in a thin reef of clouds far below him.

Beneath his feet the earth seemed to be leveling out. Whatever he was on he judged himself almost to the top of it. He was walking now with hands outstretched before him like a supplicant. They touched solid stone and he began to feel his way along the wall. His right arm went into what seemed to be a spherical opening he couldn't gauge the height of, a curving hallway opening off this grand ballroom, or whatever it was, but he eased inside it. The floor vanished and he was falling. He fell scrabbling wildly at insubstantial air and hit on a slanted bed of shale and fetched up against a stone wall. He rolled over feeling to see what was broken. Goddamn, he said, will you not ever learn?

He eased painfully into a sitting position with his back against the wall and rolled up his pants leg. He could feel blood trickling down his leg into his soggy shoe and his fingers found a ragged cut but he couldn't find any broken bones. He crossed his arms over his knees and laid his head on them. He figured to rest awhile and then go on but he was wearier than he'd known. He fell asleep and dreamed.

Up from the black maw of dark they came, a gaudy procession of coppercolored folk begarbed in garments of flax dyed all manner of color by berries. Their ceremonial robes were stained with bark and blood and they were materializing before the ebony mouth and taking their places with serene solemnity. Another one magically appearing out of the vortex of nothingness and following singlefile a path trod out of riotous greenery with, on all sides, a rising cacophony of exotic birdcalls, the strangelooking birds themselves moving above them

*left to right like stageprops strung on wires and the line
of men advancing upon him with their gold bracelets
and anklets winking off the sun with a solemn silence as
if this had all been agreed upon before and was simply
a matter of form.*

*He stirred himself where he lay. The sun was a ma-
lefic weight he struggled under. The hot damp air tinged
with solidity that restrained him. They were upon him, he
could smell their rank greased bodies, see their pocked
faces leaning toward his own when they lifted him from
the earth. They bore him through the jungle before them
like an offering and when he inquired of them their des-
tination, their speech was guttural and foreign and their
faces as solemn and expressionless as pallbearers moving toward the graveyard with the dead.*

*The one clearing the way slashed the cane and
grasses with a copper broadsword and the air grew thick
with shredded greenery. Strange broadleaved trees of an
incredible hue of green from whose high branches garish dayglo birds, like the opulent output of lunatic taxi-
dermists, watched them pass with eyes of ebony glass.
Everywhere was a dense wall of bracken and vines and
brush beyond which an exotic life thrived and he could
hear the soft padding of jaguar and the furtive movement of serpents and when they crested a hill and he
could see around him the world fell away in lush opulent
horizons and valleys between the hills from which thick
mist rose and the world looked atavistic and unherald-
ed. Time so new that such primitive folk as these did not
even bother to measure it.*

*Descending now, horizons choppy with some man-
ner of palmtrees, below them a series of temples shaped
like truncated pyramids, an unreckonable number of
them that tended away into distance. A dead city of the*

jungle in its infancy. They went on, following a stone-floored thoroughfare, the village became a city with folk falling back deferentially. This strange procession then falling into loose ranks following Crowe to the heart of the city and to some fate that filled him with dread.

The clearer of the way gestured wordlessly to an arched stone opening in the temple, an enormous single block of limestone with a floodgroove chiseled into its surface. They entered the pyramid wherein lay another smaller pyramid with a glittering surface of limitless ground and they had lit torches that flared unwavering in the windless hallway and there were other torches set in sconces as they ascended stairways built into the space between the pyramids, stone stairways that were ancient even then with depressions worn by millions of sandalled feet. The fourth stairway opened onto the flattened top of the pyramid and they ushered him into the sunlight onward toward a glittering throne marvelously veneered with gold leaf hammered thin and set with rubies and all fell back save the executioner at his side.

Above him a diminutive childking in robes of pale linen and adorned with ornate jewelry and stone obelisks and about his throat a disc of hammered gold whereon were hieroglyphs of the image of a god more barbaric than any god that ever was. He was unsheathing a sacrificial dagger intricately chipped from flint. His face was hidden by a mesh of polished gold that shone like the sun itself and even as he lifted a dark child's hand to raise it, Crowe knew that he was looking at his own son.

He woke in the dark veins of the earth with his dream rising above him with the rushing of enormous wings, shivering with fear and cold and his face wet with tears.

Going upward out of the duskstained basin he felt himself at the very rim of the world and where the earth righted itself, the train was laboring westward into a world where night had not yet fallen. Remnants of the day hung gleaming before a fiery firmament and angled light crept the stubbled field as if it were seeping from whatever container imperfectly contained it. Then the burnished sky darkened like cooling metal and the remnants of fire became gray windrows of dirty looking clouds and night fell on him a second time.

Sometime after midnight, the train stopped in some city he didn't know the name of. Some big city, he had passed strings of houses, shuttered businesses, tacky honkytonks for what seemed like hours. He could hear the switchengine and hiss of air brakes and the hollow boom of cars being engaged, uncoupled and others sidetracked. Finally, they were sidetracked as well. He waited a time and got out cautiously, but he didn't see anyone about. He felt limberlegged and strange, drugged and dislocated at this clockless hour. He found another car coupled far back in some train bound east. He clambered up and already he could hear the engine and couplings, feel the little nervous jerks, and they began to move. There was wheat straw in the car and he raked it into a pile to pillow himself on and laid upon it. While they were waiting, he heard footsteps coming down the line and he held his breath. Someone checking the cars. He heard the door of the one next slide, after a moment slam to. A flashlight clicked on and pinned him where he was frozen in cold white light, trapped like an animal, pinned like a specimen on a slide. There was a small apprentice

engineer behind the roundfaced man in a striped rail-
roaders cap. In the rim of the light's glare his face was
orange and sinister as a jack-o-lantern. He watched them
for a moment then the light clicked off and he turned.
He could hear him whistling, his footfalls diminishing in
the gravel, could see the light moving jerkily along the
ground beside him like some phosphorescent pet capering at his feet.

The train shot on into the night with the headlight
burning away the dark as cleanly as an arc welder. The
city fell away like dirty papers in a slipstream and after awhile they were climbing east into the mountains,
barren fields stitched together by looping wires on tele-
graph poles. A great white moon had arisen and paced
them behind a horizon of jagged black rock. Interpreted
by wonder, the fields and woods ran surreal and alien
in the moonlight, Rorschach clumps of trees stood out
far down in the gorges, inkbordered streams that crept
the dark rock like quicksilver and everything he saw was
touched with an unearthly beauty.

A constant dervish of straw whirlwinded about the
car. At first he picked the straw out of his hair but as the
train accelerated he was in a veritable sandstorm of it and
he just covered his face with a palm until most of it blew
away and after awhile he slept.

They are gone now, vanished to the last man. They are
dust and fluted bone in grownover graveyards, their eyes
burn out of yellowing daguerreotypes in the bottom of

forgotten pitted faces and their names taste foreign on the tongue, chalky, dry as dust. Even their feeble scrawlings on the earth have been taken by the timer. The very fabric of their lives is as lost as they are. Their land, scrub blackjack and pine.

Their seed mutated and spread on a thousand virulent strains to the cities of the industrial north, they took to the tacky little factory towns like a plague. They bred on backroads and neon allnight honkytonks and festered in secondhand housetrailers. They perish unmourned, on poolroom floors and in the twisted metal of cars on bloody highways.

Only the old houseplaces endure. Their foundation rocks stand like monuments of some fallen and prior race and the myths of these old gods are transcribed only in shards of blue bottleglass and the working silence of the dark unmetered poets.

They had moved across the earth as briefly as the passage of the sun, then they were gone and all there was to mark their tenancy were random hieroglyphics, senseless and insignificant as a chicken's scratching in the dust. Then the wind rose and that was gone too.

Nothing but the earth endures.

THE END

Postscript
by J. M. White

Fugitives of the Heart is the last major work from William Gay's archives. When William died in 2012 a small group of his friends started working to bring the unpublished material into print. The archive included *The Lost County, Little Sister Death, Stoneburner,* and now *Fugitives of the Heart.* There are still some unpublished short stories, enough to make a nice collection, and then a novel he wrote when he was twenty-five years old.

William's trajectory as a writer did not come into focus until after he died. During his lifetime people associated him with Southern literature and mostly with William Faulkner. However, now that his whole body of work is available, it is obvious that he wrote novels in each of the genres that he loved to read. He read anything and everything: magazines, fiction, non-fiction, poetry, whatever he could get his hands on. But, of course, he had his favorites, William Faulkner and Cormac McCarthy certainly had the greatest influence, but he read it all. He liked Davis Grubb and read even the trashy Southern literature. Along with these, he loved Gothic horror and ghost stories. He was impressed how a good ghost story could give you the willies and how you could be horrified by the darkness and death portrayed in a Gothic tale. And he read the hard-boiled detective stories, especially Ross Macdonald, but any of them would do.

He ran across Mark Twain before he read any Faulkner since he had access to Twain at his school and got to read *Tom Sawyer* and then *The Adventures of Huckleberry Finn.* Here was literature about kids he could relate to, kids living in the country and the thrill of reading it never left him. As an adult he was fond of quoting from the first page of *Huck Finn* where Huck is describing how this writer had written a story about his friend Tom Sawyer and Huck remarked that the story was mostly true but that it had "a few stretchers." When William quoted those lines, he would do so with a little grin on his face and, as I got to know him, I learned that he took it to heart that it was part of the writer's craft to use a few stretchers.

Fugitives of the Heart is his homage to Mark Twain. It is his Huck Finn story set in his own mythic geography of the Harrikin and Ackermann's Field, in rural Lewis County, Tennessee. But the elements of the Twain story are there, the orphan living on his own whose best friend is a Black man, and then to top it off there is a scene in a cave near the end of the book. There you have it, playing out the Twain themes in his own way, in his own voice. *Fugitives of the Heart* includes a passage that makes his appreciation of Mark Twain crystal clear. When the main character in the novel, Yates, is living with the widow she reads to him from *Huckleberry Finn*, telling him,

It's the greatest novel an American ever wrote, she told him. She thought a while. Or any other nationality, she added.

And, just as *Fugitives of the Heart* is his homage to Mark Twain, *Stoneburner* is his homage to the hard-boiled detective story, *Little Sister Death* is his ghost story, and *Twilight* his Gothic novel. *The Long Home* was written under the influence of Cormac McCarthy while *The Lost County* and *Provinces of the Night* pay homage to Faulkner who showed him you could write truly great literature, world class literature, set in the rural South.

I heard about William and read *Provinces of Night*. I was coming on a work assignment to Hohenwald where William lived, and I decided to look him up. I quickly learned that he loved to talk about Cormac McCarthy. I had read *All the Pretty Horses* but that was all, so William immediately recommended *Suttree*. I ordered a copy and when I read it, I was impressed starting on page one. We had many long discussions going over different parts of the book. He knew it intimately and relished talking about it. I was blown away by the language and by the story telling and once, when I remarked to William how impressed I was with McCarthy's use of language, and how he seemed to make the readers aware of events without ever describing them in the text, William said that if I wanted to know where Cormac had learned it I should read Faulkner's *The Hamlet*. I had read some of Faulkner in college English classes and knew that Faulkner's influence on William's writing was even greater than McCarthy's. I went out and got a copy of *The Hamlet* and quickly read through it. All the things that I had been praising so highly in Cormac's writing were there. I was shocked. It was like a template that McCarthy had absorbed and used to write *Suttree*. I had been praising McCarthy for being an innovator, for being wildly creative with his language and now it turned out that he had learned it nearly verbatim from Faulkner. Now I understood William's obeisance to Faulkner.

Of the seven novels that William wrote, only three were published during his lifetime. Much of his unpublished writing existed as handwritten notebooks and most of these were stored in the attic of the house where he raised his kids. William's literary aesthetic was such that once he wrote something, he was done with it. He always had a new story, a new novel he was working on and he was not one to go back and dig up something he had written years before. The creative impulse dictated what he should do and to look back at things he had done was a waste of time and a drain of the energy that could be poured into a new story, a new novel. Consequently, there was a horde of unpublished material hidden away in the attic of the house he had moved out of many years before. Luckily his daughter was living in the house, raising another generation of kids, so the notebooks and manuscripts were safe there. And it was only after all these notebooks written during the decades of the 1970s, 1980s and 1990s were discovered that the full dimensions of his life as a writer came into view.

Writing was his passion, it was all he cared about, everything else was secondary. By the time he got published at age fifty-nine he had been writing for over thirty years. He was fascinated by the written word. He was weirdly, wildly out of place, growing up in extreme poverty, living in a two-room shack on a farm where the rent was paid in farm labor. He had little access to books. When he found his first dictionary, he read it from cover to cover. There was a small library in his high school and he once asked the librarian how much she had to pay for the privilege of working in the library. One of his high school teachers noticed that he was reading all the time and gave him a book by Faulkner and one by Thomas Wolfe. He read them at night by the light of a kerosene lamp. Here were writers he could admire, that he could learn from, that he could emulate. Things would never be the same after that.

His parents never owned a car, never had electricity, heated with wood, used kerosene lamps for light, and had an outhouse out back. He knew he wanted to write from the time he knew anything. There were no books in the house, neither his father nor mother were readers, they didn't even have a pencil or pen in the house. At age twelve, he got a notebook and sharpened a stick and made his own ink out of walnut stain and started writing. He filled the notebook from front to back, then turned it over, and filled the back of the pages from back to front, a habit he maintained for the rest of his life, writing mostly in spiral bound notebooks that he bought at the local drug stores. Those first pages still exist in the William Gay archive, now located at Sewanee University.

He wrote his first novel at age twenty-five. He would send off handwritten stories to magazines until he figured out that he had to get them typed before they would even read them. He acquired a typewriter but never advanced beyond two-finger pecking and continued to write in longhand. By age thirty-five he had honed his style and was at the height of his powers, and he knew it. But, at the same time, no one was buying; he would submit stories and novels only to get rejection slip after rejection slip. Occasionally he would get a note with the rejection slips saying they liked his work, but his language was too poetic, too lyrical and that if he would just re-write in a more straight-forward way they would consider publishing him. But that was not about to happen. He had spent hard years learning to write with his own unique voice and he was not about to compromise. He recognized his own genius even if no one else did. He set a standard to write as well as Faulkner, as well as Cormac McCarthy, and by God he was there. He set a high bar and didn't stop until he reached it. It set him apart, especially in rural Lewis County, Tennessee. The only person he had to talk with was his younger brother Cody. Cody would read his stories as quickly as he wrote them. But the rest of the people in his circle were barely educated, even by the standards of Lewis County and couldn't care less about lyrical realism or anything literary. It made him seem stand-offish, he was separated from the population-at-large by a great gulf.

He was constantly watching for new books and he ran across Cormac McCarthy's first novel, *The Orchard Keeper*, soon after its publication. Once he started reading it, he recognized McCarthy's genius and watched for all Cormac's subsequent books. He knew from the blurbs on the dust jackets that Cormac lived in Knoxville and one day, on a whim, he called the operator and asked if she had a listing for Cormac McCarthy in Knoxville. He was totally surprised when the operator gave him a number. He called it and was in shock when McCarthy answered the phone. William had a very distinctive accent and Cormac must have recognized immediately that he was talking to someone from the country. They started corresponding and eventually Cormac asked William if he had ever written anything and, when he learned that William was a writer, he invited him to send a few pages to review. William was working on an early draft of *Provinces of Night* and had his daughter type up a few pages and Cormac read them with interest, marked them up and sent them back. William treasured those pages and would show them to visitors if they were fans of Cormac. Cormac was writing *Suttree* at the time and as a sign of his recognition of William's talent, he sent a manuscript copy to William before it was published. William read through it twice and faithfully returned it.

Finally, at age fifty-nine, he published two short stories, almost simultaneously. One of the magazine editors was associated with a small press in Denver. He called William and asked if he had a novel they could consider for publication. It was a story William was fond of telling and he would get a sly furtive look on his face and say,

"And of course I did." As if any reasonable person would have a full-length novel laying around ready to submit at a call from a publisher. It just so happened that he had both *The Long Home* and *Provinces of Night* basically ready to go. He chose *The Long Home* and it was published the next year. Suddenly a degree of fame descended on him, and where he had seemed arrogant to the local redneck population, to the literary elite he seemed humble and self-effacing.

It is interesting to note that William was not only a literary artist, he also loved to paint. He started painting as a teen-ager when someone gave him a paint-by-number set for Christmas. It had a drawing of a clown on it with the sections of the clown's face marked with numbers that showed you what colors to use. William turned the canvas board over and painted a train crossing a high trestle on the back. His paintings often illustrate the themes in the books, he used dark pallets and most of his paintings reflect the haunting, dark, mysterious, settings in which he places his characters.

He lived as much of his life as possible in a writer's trance. When he was forced to work, he tried to do jobs where he was off to himself doing repetitive work, so he could free his mind to plot out whatever he was writing at the time. He would concentrate his attention and watch as the story developed like a dream or a fantasy, replaying the scenes, trying different variations, then, that evening after work, he would take an old kitchen chair out to the edge of the woods and sit there and write what he had seen that day, and by this time he knew, nearly word for word, what he was going to write. That was what he lived for.

I got to know his ex-wife Diane after he died. Her lament, the first time I met her, and ever after, was that he would not work, that all he wanted to do was write. She had lived with him for many years and he would stay home writing until the bills piled up and the wolves were howling at the door. Then, and only then, he would go out and get a job, hanging sheetrock, painting houses or working in a local factory, until he made enough to pay the bills. Then he would quit and sit at home reading and writing all day. It drove her crazy. She was trying to hold the family together with six mouths to feed and it seemed to her that he was just not doing his part and there was nothing she could do to make him act any different. In William's mind, his writing was his real work. The problem was his writing didn't earn him a dime until he was nearly sixty years old and, by that time, he was long divorced from Diane, who had given up on him.

For William, those moments, when he was daydreaming, when he was plotting out his stories, and when he was sitting at the edge of the woods, a notebook on his knee, writing with a pencil, they were his real work and that was the only thing that validated him and gave him his sense of worth. He was the only person who knew he was a genius, his wife didn't see it, his kids eventually came to recognize it but only much later in life, his friends didn't have a clue, many of them considered him an aloof smart-ass. But those moments when the story appeared, when that string of words flowed and the characters played through their dialogues, these were the moments he lived for and he was very familiar with them, had them pretty much at his command, and was doing it, regardless of what anyone thought. This was what he had worked all his life to do and, for him, there was nothing else worth doing, it was a treasure worth far more than the coin of the realm.

And along with this he developed the ability to tell

the untold tale. He was able to have the reader understand
what was happening in a story without ever mentioning
it or describing it as it was occurring. It is quite a literary
tour-de-force as the reader becomes aware of something
after the fact and figures out some important component
of the plot without the writer ever telling that part of the
story. These untold tales are revealed by the consequences
that follow inevitably in their wake. He gives a clue about
this in *Fugitives* when he says,

> the past and present intersected
> seamlessly and he saw how there was no
> true beginning or end and that all things
> once done were done forever and went
> spiraling outward fainter and fainter like
> ripples on water and that the face of a
> young girl carried at once within her a
> bitter harridan and past that the satinpil-
> lowed deathbed of the grave.

This makes unusual demands on the reader who
gradually must figure out what has happened in the untold
parts. These untold tales become evident because they are
necessary to shape the present moment of the book since
you could not get to where you are without those events.

William's writing explodes with epiphanous language rich in poetic description. His unique lyrical realism
is as if Rimbaud had taken to novel writing. His prose is
filled with phrases that twist your mind using unexpected
words to paint scenes that are startling in their originality,
that intuitively transport the reader. The imagistic revela-
tory prose marks him as one of the consummate literary
artists of our time. His prose is filled with passages that
hit some neuro-aesthetic circuit in the brain and create the

same type of experience you feel when you are standing in front of a work of art in a museum. His writing comes at you intense with literary creativity. This made him a writer's writer, for many years widely acclaimed by the literati but largely unrecognized by the public at large. Now, as the unpublished works are coming into print, the full picture of his life as a writer will come into view.

BIBLIOGRAPHY

Novels:

The Long Home, MacMurray and Beck, Denver, CO, 1999

The Long Home, Faber and Faber, London, England, 1999

La demeure eternelle, Editions du Seuil, France, 2012

Provinces of Night, Doubleday, New York, NY, 2000

Provinces of Night, Faber and Faber, London, England, 2000

Provinzen der Nacht, Argon Verlag GmbH, Berlin, Germany, 2001

Twilight, MacAdam/Cage, San Francisco, CA, 2006

Twilight, Faber and Faber, London, England, 2007

Crepuscolo, Gea Schiro Editore, Italy, 2009

La mort au crepuscule, Gallimard, France, 2010

Schemer, Omslag Dog & Pony, Amsterdamn, 2015

Little Sister Death, Dzanc Books, Ann Arbor, MI, 2015

Stoneburner, Anomolaic Press, Brush Creek, TN, 2018

Stoneburner, Editions Gallimard, France, 2018

Stoneburner, Polar Verlag SmbH, Germany, 2019

The Lost County, Dzanc Books, Ann Arbor, MI, 2018

The Lost Country, Faber and Faber, England. 2019

Novellas:

The Paperhanger, the Doctor's Wife and the Child

Who Went into the Abstract, The Book Source, Hohenwald, TN, 1999

Come Home, Come Home, It's Suppertime, The Book Source, Hohenwald, TN, 2000

Short Story Collections:

I Hate to See that Evening Sun Go Down, The Free Press, New York, NY, 2002

Wittgenstein's Lolita and The Iceman, Wild Dog Press, Brush Creek, TN 2006

Time Done Been Won't Be No More, Wild Dog Press, Brush Creek, TN 2010

Short Story Publications:

"Those Deep Elm Brown's Ferry Blues," (*Missouri Review,* Fall 1998)

"I Hate to See that Evening Sun Go Down," (*Georgia Review,* Fall 1998)

"Closure and Roadkill on the Life's Highway," (*Atlantic Monthly,* November 1999)

"The Paperhanger," (*Harpers,* February 2000)

"A Death in the Woods," (*GQ,* November 2000)

"My Hand is Just Fine Where It Is," (*Oxford American,* September October 1999)

"The Crimper," (Harpers, October 2000)

"Good Til Now," (*Oxford American,* January February 2001)

"Charting the Territories of the Red," (*Southern Review* Spring 2001)

"Homecoming" in Stories from the Blue Moon Cafe II: Anthology of Southern Writers, Edited by Sonny Brewer, MacAdams Cage, 2003.

"Wreck on the Highway," (*Chattahoochee Review*, 2005)

"Where Will You Go When Your Skin Cannot Contain You," (*Tin House*, 2007)

Articles

"Sweet Songs Never Last Too Long," (*Oxford American, Music Issue*, July August 1999)

"Queen of the Haunted Dell," (*Oxford American* October 2000)

"Sitting on Top of the World," (*Oxford American Music Issue* 2000)

"Time Done Been Won't Be No More," (*Oxford American, July/August Music Issue*, 2001)

"Crossroads Blues," (*Oxford American* 2002, website only)

"Blind Willie McTell," (*Oxford American*, Summer, 2005)

"Calves Howling at the Moon," (*Oxford American*, Fall, 2005)

"The Man in the Attic: A Memoir," (*Paste*, June/July, 2006)

"The Banjo Man," (*Oxford American*, Music Issue, Summer, 2006)

"Fumbling for the Keys to the Doors of Perception: A memoir, mostly true but with some stretchers, as Mark Twain once said," in *Don't Quit Your Day Job: Acclaimed Authors and the Day Jobs They Quit* Edited by Sonny Brewer, M P Publishing Limited, (2010)

"Introduction," *As I Lay Dying* by William Faulkner, Illustrations by Katherine Hardy, London, The Folio Society, 2011.

"Reading the South," (Paperback Edition), (*Chatta-*

hoochee Review, Volume XXXI, Number 3, Winter, 2011)

Anthologies:

New Stories from The South, The Year's Best, edited by Shannon Ravenel, 1998,

New Stories from The South, The Year's Best, edited by Shannon Ravenel, 1999

New Stories from The South, The Year's Best, edited by Shannon Ravenel, 2000

Best New American Voices, edited by Tobias Wolff, 2000

New Stories from The South, The Year's Best, edited by Shannon Ravenel, 2001

O'Henry Prize Stories, edited by Larry Dark, 2001

Best Mystery Stories, edited by Lawrence Block, 2001

Best Music Writing, edited by Nick Hornby, 2001

New Stories from The South, The Year's Best, edited by Shannon Ravenel, 2002

Stories From the Blue Moon Café, edited by Sonny Brewer, 2002

Stories from the Blue Moon Cafe II, edited by Sonny Brewer, 2003

They Write Among Us, edited by Jim Dees, 2003

Stories from the Blue Moon Cafe III, edited by Sonny Brewer, 2004

Anchor Book of Modern Short Stories, edited by Ben Marcus, 2004

Stories from the Blue Moon Cafe IV, edited by Sonny Brewer, 2004

Best of the South: The Best of the Second Decade, selected by Anne Tyler, 2005

A Cast of Characters and Other Stories, edited by

Sonny Brewer, 2006

Best American Short Stories, edited by Steven King, 2007

Best American Mystery Stories, edited by Carl Hiaasen, 2007

The Surreal South, edited by Pinckney Benedict, 2007

The Ecco Anthology of Contemporary American Short Fiction, edited Joyce Carol Oates and Christopher R. Beha, 2008

Grit Lit: A Rough South Reader, edited by Brian Carpenter and Tom Franklin, 2012

Editor

With Suzanne Kingbury, *The Alumni Grill,* MacAdam Cage, 2004.

Interviews:

William Gay offers a piercing portrait of a vanishing rural culture: Interview by Alden Mudge, *BookPage,* January, 2001.

Out of Nowhere: After decades of laboring in complete obscurity, Middle Tennessee author William Gay has finally found literary acclaim, by Clay Risen: *Nashville Scene*, January 16, 2003 p 23 – 27.

A Natural Talent: Author William Gay, snug amid woods of his native Hohenwald, reflects on lifelong love of words. By Julie Gillen, *The Daily Herald,* Sunday, March 7, 2004, 1D, 4D. Columbia, TN.

An Interview with William Gay by Georgia Afton, *Water-Stone Review: A Literary Annual,* Volume 7, Fall 2004, p. 42-59.

Monday Interview: William Gay, Things I'd Rather be Doing, 3.26.2007

Bookmark with Don Noble, Interview with William Gay, Produced by The Center for Public Television at the University of Alabama (c) 2007 by University of Alabama Center for Public Television (DVD)

Interview William Gay, Tennessee Literary Project, MTSU, Conducted by Kenny Torrella, April 13, 2008, www.mtsu.edu/tnlitproj

Inventing Tennessee's own Yoknapatawpha County by Clay Risen, 10/2009, Tennessee Committee for the Humanities www.chapter16.org

William Gay: Featured Writer of the Month, November, 2009, *Oxford American* www.oxfordamerican. org/interviews/2009/nov/04/featured-writer-month/

Positively William Gay, Interviewed by Anthony Scarlati, *Nashville Arts Magazine*, December 2009, P. 27 – 31.

Ackerman's Field and Lewis County: Lewis County author William Gay's stories to hit the big screen. By Jordan Blie, *Lewis County Herald*, January 7, 2010. p. 1, p. 5.

Awards:

1999 William Peden Award
1999 James A. Michener Memorial Prize
2002 Guggenheim Fellowship
2007 United States Artists Ford Foundation Fellow
2009 Writer of the Year, Tennessee Literary
    Association
2010 *Grand Priz de Litterature Policiere* for *Twilight*

Acknowledgements

A special thanks goes to William's family: his children William Gay, Jr., Chris Gay and Lee Gay, and to his brother Cody Gay. Shelia Kennedy and Susan McDonald worked tirelessly typing and editing the manuscript. An incredible team of other volunteers came together including Lamont Ingalls, Editor Emeritis of Anomolaic Press, and Paul Nitsche, web master of the William Gay archive webpage and graphic designer for William's publications with Anomolaic Press, who were both involved at every phase of this and all the previous books. Others who worked on editing and proofing for this project include Matt Snope, a university professor who teaches William's books in his classes, Dawn Major, who wrote her MFA thesis on William's work, George Dilworth, a dedicated reader, and Coree Entwistle, my daughter.

Lamont Ingalls, a native of Middle Tennessee, has been glad to continue to work with wild dog/Anomolaic Press during this decade-long effort to recover, edit and publish the masterful prose of William Gay. He is looking forward to editing additional literary treasures recovered from the attic in Lewis County.

Synopsis (by William Gay)

Fugitives of the Heart is a novel of a boy's coming of age in a dying iron ore mining community of Depression era Tennessee. Marion Yates has a hardscrabble and violent existence, but you wouldn't believe it if you knew him. He's too busy breaking into life to feel sorry for himself. His father died when he was a child and his mother is a sometimes prostitute who neglects and offhandedly abuses him and food is hard to come by, but hard times are on the land everywhere and everyone has their own sad tales to tell.

He has an ongoing and bitter war with an old lady bootlegger named Granny Stovall. This war is escalated when he falls in love with the old woman's granddaughter. The novel progresses by episodes which, while self-contained, move the narrative along. He hitches a ride on an ore train to Ackerman's Field, the nearest town, for a darkly comic visit to a circus. When his mother dies, he is taken in by the young widow Paiton but this doesn't last long and soon he is back on his own.

The main narrative of the novel concerns Yates and a free-spirited independent black man named Crowe. Crowe befriends Yates and earns a fierce undying loyalty but, when Yates helps him escape a mob bent on hanging him, Crowe ultimately betrays him.

By the novel's end the mining operation has shut down; it has become economically unfeasible to mine the ore. Folks who are able are leaving, the rest just continuing their struggle to survive. Yates flees in a boxcar into a future which, while uncertain, is still more hopeful than the bleak and desecrated Allen's Creek community he leaves behind.

This novel takes for the setting a real place in the south-west corner of the county where I live. It was a boomtown in the 1890s and on until the mid-forties, when *Fugitives* is set. No one lives there anymore. There is nothing but mining pits and anomalaic useless looking machinery and thousands of scattered bricks from the furnace, abandoned graveyards and old houseplaces. The old houseplaces are the most evocative. Old lives seem to haunt the woods here, old voices vibrate in the air. It was while kicking through snuff glasses and broken bottles of this old community that the novel told itself to me, and I suppose I wrote it to hush those voices.

William Gay (1939-2012) lived his entire life in rural Lewis County, Tennessee, just north of the Alabama state line. He grew up in poverty and started writing with ink he made himself from walnut stain. He wrote his entire life but didn't get published until 1998 when he exploded on the literary scene. He published three novels and three collections of short stories during his life and left an archive of four unpublished novels and a collection of short stories. Two of his works have been made into films. He had four children which he raised in a hand-built home deep in the woods of Lewis County. He grew up without electricity and his parents never owned a car. He graduated from Lewis County High School and served in the Navy in Viet Nam. He worked hanging sheetrock and painting houses and wrote in the evening sitting in a beat-up chair at the edge of woods. It is remarkable that a genius of his magnitude, totally self-educated in the art of writing, came out of the backwoods of rural Tennessee.